PRAISE FOR GREGORY WILLIAMS

"These are stories about the boundaries of love, and how terrifying it can be to face up to our own emotional shortcomings."

— CLINT MCCOWN

"…a multi-layered, deeply human, and emotionally forensic collection of stories that proves hard to put down. Williams was an intrinsically talented author with a gift for nuance and observation, producing stories that veer between harsh reality and poetic magic…"

— THE BOOK REVIEW DIRECTORY

"In matters of the heart, a single lapse of judgment can prove fatal…Greg Williams is a terrific writer!"

— RON CARLSON

"These are stories that evoke laughter, even as they veer into surprise and inevitability."

— PETER SELGIN

"...steeped in the culture and arid environment of Phoenix, Arizona...Should be in any literary short story library interested in works that capture a sense of place and purpose..."

— D. DONOVAN, SR. REVIEWER,
MIDWEST BOOK REVIEW

A DRY HEAT

A Dry Heat

Collected Stories

Gregory D. Williams

Grand Canyon Press
Tempe, AZ

Grand Canyon Press
www.grandcanyonpress.com

Inside Images: Gregory Williams in a Little League uniform; the author sailing with his family; the author holding a rainbow trout (photos courtesy of the author)

Cover Images: © Евгения Юшина; artyway via www.stock.Adobe.com

Publisher's Cataloging-in-Publication (Provided by Cassidy Cataloguing Services, Inc.)

Names: Williams, Gregory D. (Gregory David), 1954-2020, author. | MacDonald, Marylee, editor.

Title: A dry heat: collected stories / Gregory D. Williams; [editor, Marylee MacDonald].

Description: Tempe, AZ: Grand Canyon Press, [2024]

Identifiers: ISBN: 978-1-951479-94-7 (paperback) | 978-1-951479-98-5 (hardback) | 978-1-951479-96-1 (Kindle) | 978-1-951479-97-8 (ePub) | 978-1-951479-99-2 (audiobook) |978-1-7320787-6-5 (audiobook)

Subjects: LCSH: Teenage boys — Fiction. | Middle-aged men — Fiction. | Widowers — Fiction. | Physicians — Fiction. | Love — Fiction. | Pain — Treatment — Fiction. | Bullies — Fiction. | Phoenix (Ariz.) — Fiction. | LCGFT: Short stories. | Linked stories. |Bildungsromans. |

BISAC: FICTION / Short Stories (single author) | FICTION / Literary. | FICTION / Coming of Age.

Classification: LCC: PS3623.I55667 D79 2024 | DDC: 813/.6 — dc23

For Linda, always and forever

It turns out you are the story of your childhood and you're under constant revision, like a lonely folktale whose invisible folks are all the selves you've been, lifelong, shadows in fog, grey glimmers at dusk.

— WILLIAM MATTHEWS

CONTENTS

FOREWORD

Real events, even minor ones, are often the springboard for fiction, and that's certainly the case with many of the stories in Gregory D. Williams' short fiction. Like the characters in two of his stories, the author drew inspiration from an idyllic childhood in Phoenix, Arizona. Like them, he played Little League, swam in backyard pools, and on warm nights climbed out on the roof to stay cool.

Gregory D. Williams, M.D. graduated from Stanford and the University of Arizona Medical School. His father was a highly regarded anesthesiologist, and the son followed in his father's footsteps. He did not start writing until after his father's untimely death. (The allegorical story, "Rainbow Trout," is the last story in this book. It was Dr. Williams' first attempt at writing fiction, and he read the story at his father's memorial service.)

His initial plunge into the creative process led Dr. Williams to enroll in online writing workshops with Nancy Packer, a retired Stanford professor and colleague of Wallace Stegner's. Eager to learn the nuts and bolts of storytelling, Williams sought out workshops with literary writers such as Robert Boswell and Ron Carlson. Close study of his favorite authors taught him how to write dramatic scenes, craft dialogue, and summarize action.

Many of the works in this collection have been previously published in literary magazines and journals. For example, "Who We Were At Twelve" was the winner of the *Arts & Letters* Fiction Prize.[1]

Here's what the story contest's final judge, Peter Selgin, had to say about the story:

> When his first (and only) novel came out in 1951, *Time's* book reviewer said of Salinger, "He can understand an adolescent mind without displaying one." I might venture a similar claim of Gregory Williams, author of "Who We Were at Twelve." While it submerged this reader thoroughly and consistently in the mindset of its pubescent characters, still, it succeeds as a sensitive, mature work of fiction in which immature pranks are underscored by deeper feelings and insights. (I was reminded, too, of Dan Pope's *In the Cherry Tree*, another work set in adolescence.) The author also displays considerable skills in carrying out a

plot that holds both surprise and inevitability, and evokes laughter even as it veers into pathos and tragedy. Lighthearted enchantment turns darkly significant as the narrator discovers "who [he was] at twelve" and — by extension — who he will be for the rest of his life.

Flying to Georgia College & State University in Milledgeville, Georgia to accept the *Arts & Letters* Prize was the highlight of the author's writing career. GCSU's famous alumna, Flannery O'Connor, lived in Milledgeville on her farm, Andalusia, and Williams was delighted to walk in her footsteps and meet the student who had pulled his manuscript from the slush pile.

In his short fiction, Williams drew on the experiences of childhood because, as all writers are told, "Write what you know." But he also drew on his knowledge of the medical profession. This is what Clint McCown, editor of *American Fiction* (New Rivers Press, 2010) had to say about "Section," another prize-winning story.

"Section" by Gregory Williams offers a convincing behind-the-scenes look at a maternity ward as an anesthesiologist struggles to cope with his fear that his own wife might give birth to a Down's Syndrome child. This is a story about the boundaries of love, and how terrifying it can be to face up to our own emotional shortcomings.

That was a feature of Williams's other medical stories. "Playing Doctor" and "What the Doctor Didn't Know" are two stories about doctors with blind spots — doctors failing to live up to the Hippocratic oath but also failing to live up to what they expected of themselves.

Williams also explored the theme of fallibility in his novel, *Open Heart*. On a surface level, *Open Heart* is a medical novel about surgeons in the "Heart Room" of a major Phoenix hospital, but at its core, it is a roman à clef about the big name doctors that the author knew personally and about the various ways we mortals allow ourselves to love and be loved. Over the course of the novel, young Gene, a flawed protagonist with a number of blind spots, must face up to his inability to fully grasp what it means to be there for another person.

However, Williams did not just mine the experiences of his childhood and his years as a doctor when he considered what to write. He was always on the lookout for a story. Wherever he went, he kept a writing notebook and recorded story ideas and snippets of dialogue. Here is what the author said about the beginnings of the story "Comps," winner of the *Bosque* Fiction Prize.

The nidus for "Comps" grew from a visit to Starbucks in 2005. As I prepared my coffee, a real-estate agent wearing a leopard-skin blouse did, in fact, say to me, "No, don't move. You're perfect." I sat near her and another man and read Ann Packer's *Mendocino* until I detected the flirtatious tone of their conversation. Then I just eavesdropped. I wrote an unsuccessful sitcom version of their dialogue that week. Later, I looked at it again, and once I discovered what George wanted — and what he feared — I had a true story.

Another story, "Three Strides to Thirty," had its origins at the Phoenix Greyhound Park. A friend in a writing workshop at Arizona State University suggested the Greyhound Park as a place that might provide grist for a story, and so a group of writers went there with the goal of seeing what kind of story might spring from such a setting. While Greg's other stories harken back to his childhood and medical career, this story, he believed, belonged in the category of "grief, regret, and things we don't talk about."

As the editor of Grand Canyon Press, I'm proud to introduce readers to an author whose focus on writing began late in life and whose life ended far too soon. Just at the start of the Covid pandemic, Greg discovered that he had an aggressive form of cancer. The cancer could not be contained. Shortly before his death, he presented a print copy of *Open Heart* to his wife Linda and their four children. *A Dry Heat*, the collection of his short fiction, completes his legacy.

Marylee MacDonald

Editor, Grand Canyon Press

---

1. "Who We Were at Twelve" first appeared in *Arts & Letters*, Vol. 24, Fall 2010.

PART I

YOUTH

CALL OF THE WOLF

PROSE POEM

I've been living with a wolf spider for five days now. At first, he stayed high over the window in my study, preening, weighing his options like a mercenary on leave. The furry triple-jointed legs and the bolt-cutter mouth stirs an ancient repulsion in me, an instinct to swat him. But the thought of crushing something the size of a paper Mai Tai umbrella gives me the willies. Besides, somewhere I learned that he was harmless, that unless you were a black widow, a cockroach, or a scorpion, you had nothing to fear. I could research the legend, but I might be wrong and I need an ally.

Today, he rests at eye level on the bottom slat of the shutters like some eight-legged cowboy sitting on a fence — one leg stretched out, seven legs up. Content. At some point he'll simply crawl away. It could be thirst, or hunger. Maybe the jungle of the bougainvillea will be too tempting. Or perhaps on a whim — or a calling — he'll sail to Japan to duel Godzilla, saving the townspeople from certain annihilation.

Oh, the things I could do with eight legs.

ROUNDING THE BASES

I t's only a bunt, but that little "tick" off the bat sounds as sweet as a double down the line. My first hit during a game this season. Kelly Barrett, the best ballplayer in eighth grade, has been working with me. I did it just like she said: *Catch the ball with the bat.* She's sitting behind the fence along the first base line.

I'm kind of her project for the summer. As I walk back to the bag she says, "Fundamentals, Willie. It's all about fundamentals." I've been hearing that a lot from her lately. Mr. Helfinstine, our coach, calls out, "Last batter." He takes his cap off, wipes his large forehead with a handkerchief, and then looks at the thermometer he looped on the fence. He's got this thing about not keeping us out past one hundred degrees.

It's Saturday, the season's two weeks old, and there aren't any games next week because of graduation. Later today, I'm going with Kelly and her dad to the batting cage. But for now, we've got this practice game going. We're playing the Apaches, and I feel bad for them. They're not very good. They don't even get to have the name of a real team, like Cubs or Dodgers or the Giants, the name of my team.

Moose Parker is up next. His real name is Randy, a big redheaded kid with freckles and glasses. He's our best pitcher, makes the all-stars every year, and today, he has already mashed one over the Michael's Mortuary section of the left field fence. Peter Bailey, another all-star, waits on deck. He used to be called Booger Bailey for a bad habit he had in fifth grade. I don't know another kid that could have outgrown that nickname. Hitting line drives will do that for you.

I take a lead: my legs are flexed, I'm on the balls of my feet, my arms relaxed — Kelly's fundamentals — the things we worked on last weekend. When the pitcher throws over, I make it back standing.

Kelly cups her hands to her mouth. "Bigger lead. Take one more step."

This is my first year in the Senior League and probably my last. Ninth graders can play but most don't come back. I hear things change once high school starts. She wants me to "play to my strengths." She says things like that. The girl's like a scout.

I'm sure she gets it from her dad, like she got that tiny gap between her front teeth and the way her toes kind of point in when she walks and maybe some of that bossiness, too. We've had four games so far and Kelly summed me up this way last weekend: Good fielder at second base. Quick hands. Makes diving stops. Overmatched at the plate. Can't hit his weight. (I only weigh a hundred pounds, so that kind of hurt.) Fast. Could lead the league in steals if he can get on base.

I take that extra step, then another as the pitcher throws over twice more. Now, I'm far enough away so that when I dive back, I'm laid out, my head turned away and my hand touching the back corner of the bag. It's what she showed me. From the dugout, Ed Guerin, our catcher yells, "Run on him, Willie. This guy's a pud." Kids tend to do what Ed says. He acts like a tough guy, raises up on his toes when he walks, but he and I have always gotten along. When I look at Kelly, she's got her arms folded. It's our steal sign. She thinks the pitcher is going to the plate. Mr. Helfinstine's not giving me anything. He's checking his thermometer and getting itchy.

I go on the pitcher's first move. A good jump. The second baseman moves over. He's straddling the bag, his glove arm aimed at the catcher. Moose has taken the pitch. When I slide, it's not like I've said to myself *slide now*. I just do it and it comes naturally, but not naturally enough. I land on the outside of my right knee and ankle. The rubber cleats of my left shoe catch a rut in the ground from when kids ride bikes through the field during irrigation. I'm tossed onto my face like I've been shot out of a catapult, Wylie Coyote style, a good two feet shy of the bag.

I sit up. My eyes are blurry, but I can see blood on my white T-shirt. Crying is not an option. I'm no pantywaist. The other team's coach is saying he doesn't think it's broken, and I know he means my nose. I wipe my eyes and see Kelly there on one knee among the players.

"Are you okay?" Mr. Helfinstine tilts my head back and pinches my nose with something soft.

I nod yes as best I can.

Kelly says, "Don't worry, we'll work on it."

With her help, Mr. Helfinstine loads my bike into his car. He insists on driving me home, saying I need to get those scrapes cleaned up and get some ice on my beak right away. Kelly comes around to the window. "I'll tell my dad you're taking a rain check on the batting cage."

Mom's the doctor at our house. Not a real doctor, but she's got a routine about certain things, and unless she comes to my dad for something, he sticks to his accounting business. My face gets a good wash. Then she prescribes the triple threat: Bactine, ice, and rest. She knows I've got a graduation speech to give in four days, "Young America, It's Up to You," and now added to her concern that I'm not practicing my speech enough, she's worried that I'll look like a raccoon Wednesday night.

Mr. Estes, my English teacher, chose Jill Butterfield and me to give speeches. Jill and her twin brother Geoffrey (a nice guy, but I've never seen him play ball) live on Kelly's street. Estes gave me the topic and some suggestions. He knew I liked baseball and thought I should put a few baseball sayings in my speech. Our class has been building a list of them on the chalkboard since Opening Day this season; things like "get in there and pitch," "the big time," and "touch all the bases" — everyday sayings that people borrowed from baseball. You get five points extra credit for each one.

We have over fifty so far. Ed keeps adding "boner," which really did come from baseball, but Mr. Estes keeps erasing it. Estes is okay, though. Last fall he brought in a TV and gave us a choice: seventh game of the World Series or continue our discussion of *Animal Farm*. It was unanimous. He's big on democracy.

Kelly calls the next day, wants me to come over. She has an idea about my batting stance she needs to show me. I tell her I can't. My mom's got a two-day icing protocol going, and she doesn't want me doing anything that could worsen the purple haze spreading across my nose and under my eyes. So Kelly comes over to my house and promises my mom she'll rotate the ice while we listen to the Dodgers' game. She doesn't show me the stance though; says she needs a bat and some space. It's always a production with her.

The Dodgers' game was my idea. They're Kelly's favorite team and the only one you can pick up on the radio in Arizona. I'm a Giants fan. Normally I wouldn't listen to an LA game unless they were playing San Francisco, but something special may be happening and I want to follow it through. Don Drysdale, the Dodgers ace, has pitched three shutouts in a row. The National League record is four. The major league record is five. If he gets to six, he'll be the first. And if that happens, it will be the first major league *first* that has occurred while I've been keeping the book.

It's not a book really, more like a list, although it's going to be a book someday. It's a bunch of baseball firsts that I've heard from announcers on the radio or NBC's *Game of the Week*. I started keeping it so I could stump Kelly. Some are weird things. *First brothers to bat in order: Felipe, Matty, and Jesus Alou, San Francisco, September 10, 1963.* It gave us something to talk about last fall during dance lessons at a place called Junior Assembly. Kelly and I learned the waltz and the fox trot with enough space between us to fit "a volleyball and a conversation," as the lady put it. We twirled around an hour a week for about a month. We even won a few ribbons, but Kel almost never got the answers to my questions. Occasionally, I'd make one up and just lob it in to her: *First teacher at Citrus Groves Elementary School to let his class watch a World Series Game: Mr. Estes, fourth period English, October 12, 1967.* She got it right, but she gave me a look. She had Estes second period — before the game started. Boy, was she jealous. She's present for another kind of first tonight, though. Between her trips to the kitchen to refill the bag with crushed ice for my nose, Don Drysdale gets his shutout, five-zip over the Astros. Two more to go for the record. It's the first time she's ever heard me root for the Dodgers.

I've known Kelly since third grade. She was in my homeroom when Mrs. Guest caught me listening to one of the Giants'-Yankees' games during the 1962 World Series. I was using an earpiece. The transistor radio was inside my desk. Sometime after that, Kelly started calling me Willie instead of Charlie. It's short for Willingham, but she also knew that Willie Mays was my favorite player. She and I played on the same Farm League team that year. Her dad coached our team, and Kel was the best kid in the league. After that she had to play softball. But she doesn't play like a girl. She throws like a guy, hits like a guy, and runs like a guy. I have one of the fastest times in the fifty, but she beats me going away. She's like a gazelle. Except for English and Math, she beats me in just about everything. I know she's taller too, maybe an inch over me right now, but I might be catching up. A couple months ago Ed measured me during Shop. I was pretty sure I was over five feet. The mark's still there on the doorjamb. Of course, Ed didn't use a pencil. He scratched it with a screwdriver, through the paint, through the primer, right into the steel. When he dropped a tape to the line, it read five feet one and one-half inches. I've grown a little since then.

The day after Drysdale's shutout, Kelly calls to see if

her ice treatments on my nose worked well enough for me to leave the house. It's Monday, Memorial Day, and neither of our families have any big plans. My mom's done what she can for my face, and now concentrates more on my speech. She makes me practice it before I head over to Kel's house. She has me stand in front of the TV while she sits straight-backed on the couch, and when I come to the last part, she puts her hands over her heart.

I take the short way to Kelly's house: through my backyard and out the back gate. All the homes along here have wood fences. She lives in the house behind mine. There's an alley that separates our homes, with an irrigation ditch about two feet deep that runs down the middle. Giant oleanders grow along one side of the ditch. They're so tall I can't even see the roof of Kelly's house from my backyard. We made a bridge over the ditch out of some old plywood and used her dad's pruning shears to cut a path through the oleanders. It's been two weeks since the last irrigation, so the ditch is dry. Before I cross the bridge, I look for baseballs that might have floated down from the city park. It's about ten houses down from us, where the alley takes a left turn. The adults use a ball field there at night, and sometimes baseballs clear the left field fence and land in the ditch.

Two summers ago, we were walking that stretch. Kelly was leading the way. She usually does. I was carrying an old pillowcase, looking hard for balls in the oleander branches. Mays had hit his five-hundredth home run the night before, and I was calculating out loud how long it would take him to reach 714, Ruth's record, when I bumped into her. She pointed into the ditch and said, "Look." It took me a second to realize I was looking at a dog, a dead dog. It wasn't too big, maybe a poodle. It was lying on its side, covered with mud, hair all plastered down. "I think it got stuck and drowned," she said.

I'd seen things dead before, but they were smaller and things you expected to see — crickets, crawdads, fish. Even birds. Saw them all the time. This was something different. I have pictures of a mutt we had when I was little, but I don't remember ever seeing it dead. It's like there were dogs and now there were dead dogs, and they were two different things. All I said was, "Poor dog." But that didn't seem like enough. We just stared at it for a while, and then without saying anything, Kelly started walking and I followed.

I was still thinking of that dog, trying to picture it alive, when Kelly yelled, "Found one!" She dug a baseball out of the mud. I think we found a couple more that day and cleaned them up. We've lost those but have found others since then. That's how it goes with baseballs.

After I cross the bridge and duck through the hole in the oleanders, I let myself in through Kelly's back gate. There are baseballs, softballs, and bats scattered all over the backyard. Drysdale, a wiry-haired dog with a beard, is doing laps in the pool, swimming under the arc of water from the aerator. Mrs. Barrett always introduces him as

"Drysdale, our Airedale." We don't have a pool, so I swim with him a lot in the summer.

Drysdale brings me a baseball. He drops it and shakes water all over me. I throw the ball down to the far end of the yard. It lands under a sailboat that Dr. Barrett has been building for so long, the grass underneath has given up. Drysdale does his combat crawl under the trailer, trying to get to the ball. Kelly said the boat's done and they're taking it down to Mexico next week on their vacation.

When I knock on the Arcadia door, Mrs. Barrett comes to the glass, wiping her hands on a towel. She's smiling until she gets closer and slides the door open. "Charlie! My goodness, what happened to you?"

I'm about to tell her how I messed up sliding into second when Kelly walks up from behind her mom. She's sipping on a can of Mountain Dew.

"He tried a head first slide," I say, taking the words right out of her mouth.

She scoots past and flips another can in the air. "Heads up."

I catch it.

"Are you okay?" her mom says. "Look at you. Oh, your poor nose. I wish Bob could see this. He just got called to the hospital." She takes my chin in the palm of her hand and tilts my face up. "Well, those scrapes will heal. Looks like you're getting a shiner, too. That'll just disappear in a few weeks. You'll be good as new." Everything always heals *good as new* in Mrs. Barrett's view. She's probably right.

"Charlie, you know Bob always says it's safer sliding feet first." She releases my chin and is back drying her hands as she heads inside. Kelly stands by the ping-pong table, bouncing a ball on the paddle. "Wanna play?" We play two out of three, but it never goes three. Holding her Mountain Dew the whole time, she beats me.

When we're done, Kelly puts Drysdale and his baseball into his pen. She grabs the first bat she sees on the way back. She squinches up her mouth — thinking.

I've seen this before. It's time to work on fundamentals. *Learn the fundamentals and everything falls into place.* That's what her dad tells her. I've heard him.

Dr. Barrett played ball in college. Kelly says the Dodgers would have signed him, but his shoulder gave out. There's a picture of him in the hallway. You pass it on the way to the bathroom. He's in a baseball uniform. He's thinner, but looks as tall as he is now. He's in the middle of his windup, his leg's real high in the air, like Juan Marichal's, and across the front of his jersey it says UCLA. There are also some pictures of Kelly and her two sisters over the years, mostly in softball uniforms. Julie goes to Arizona State and Brenda starts there next year. And there's a neat one of Kelly. She's standing between Maury Wills and her dad at a Dodgers' game. She's got a big smile on her face. Her front teeth are missing and she's holding an autographed baseball. She keeps the ball in a tube sock in her drawer now. I felt bad for her when the Dodgers traded Wills two years ago.

I first started learning about *fundamentals* the season her dad coached Kelly and me in third grade, the same year he put a cast on my wrist after I fell off the monkey bars. Now and then, I've gone over to school with Kelly and her dad to take grounders and shag flies. I've learned a bunch, and Kelly won't let me forget any of it: get your glove on the dirt to field a grounder, move forward as you catch a pop fly, run through the bag going to first. Things like that. Still, there's more he teaches her when I'm not around, and she passes that on to me. Kelly grips and re-grips the bat, really studying the *Mickey Mantle* signature on the barrel while she does it. The lesson is coming, so I pull up a patio chair and sip on my Dew.

She stands in front of me and takes a few practice swings, but they're more like a golf stroke. "Willie, before you can steal, you've got to get on base. Right?"

I've learned it's better to listen.

"Your bunting's going to be okay. That's good for a hit a game. But you're striking out way too much. We'll work on it in batting practice, but until your hitting comes around, I have an idea."

She stops swinging and leans forward on the bat. "A walk's as good as a hit. What matters is getting on base." She goes back to wheeling the bat, this time like Willie Stargell. "We need to shrink your strike zone." Now she has her legs spread wide, practically doing the splits. Kind of bent over, she's looking out past me, somewhere toward the sailboat. Waving the bat, her hands are up by her right ear.

"This is your new stance. Look at this strike zone: nipples to knees. Look how small it is."

I suppose doctors' kids are like this. She says *nipples* like I would say *armpits* and keeps right on saying whatever she was saying while looking out to some imaginary pitcher, daring him.

My head is somewhere else. The word *nipples* floats out there, lost, looking for a place to settle. I've seen nipples at Ed's house, in the stash of *Playboys* his older brother Rusty hides in the closet. Thinking about the pictures later gives me a woody. But I've never kissed a girl. Ed explained how kissing was getting to first base. Pulling into second meant you felt her boobs. Third was some kind of touching between her legs. And a home run? Ed just said, "I don't have to tell you what that is." He did have to tell me, but I didn't ask him. Anything past second base is like trying to catch a fly ball after dark — I kind of see it, but there's a chance it's going to hit me in the head.

I look at Kelly's chest. Her ASU SOFTBALL T-shirt is two sizes too big.

She's different. Even the thought of kissing her seems out in left field. She repeats, "This is it. This is your new stance. *Your* strike zone will be even smaller." She's getting really excited. "You try it."

I pose a few times, take a few swings, and she's convinced she's onto something.

"You're gonna steal a ton of bases," she says. "We'll get your sliding straightened out next time irrigation comes in, maybe after graduation."

There isn't much to the last two days of school except signing yearbooks. Most everybody writes something in mine about having a nice summer, hoping my face heals up, or seeing me at Central High next year. Kelly writes, *Willie, You're going to be the best base stealer since Maury Wills. Don't be a stranger after the season. Oh yeah, I'm the one with the pool.*

I write in hers. *Kel, Too bad you're not as good a dancer as a baseball player. We would have won more ribbons.*

The last day in Mr. Estes' class I add *raincheck* to the list on the blackboard and get the points. Then he erases it along with the fifty-four other entries, including *boner* for the last time.

On graduation night, before our principal, Mr. Wimbly, hands out the diplomas, and I stand at the podium set up along the Major League's right-field line. Behind me under the outfield lights, the Citrus Groves Elementary School eighth grade class sits on portable aluminum bleachers still warm from the sun. We're dressed in black and white. The boys have ties and every-one's hair is combed. My mom's ice protocol worked because my nose is its normal size again. Under my eyes, the purple shadows are fading at the edges. Like Mrs. Barrett promised, soon I'll be good as new.

Families sit before me in a block of perfect rows. My parents and little sister are in the front, next to Kelly's family. My speech is going well. Near the end I point to the outfield fence behind them. I explain how, on almost each section of plywood, is a name we all know: Guerin Construction, Bailey Cleaners, Roberts Furniture Gallery. I mention a few others and save Willingham and Company for last, my dad's business. That gets a few chuckles. I say that someday our names will be on those signs, and I arc my hand behind me like they do on the game shows. My mom's hands are back over her heart. Then I give my big finish. "We're heading into the big leagues now. We're rookies again, but soon we'll be old pros. There will be hard days: three strikes and you're out. But don't give up. Don't be a bench warmer. Keep swinging, and someday you'll hit one out of the park." Everyone applauds. The Barretts and my folks are particularly enthusiastic. My English teacher, Mr. Estes, is at the end of the front row giving me the thumbs-up.

Two days later, my mom takes me to the library downtown. Drysdale's record has got me thinking about other possible pitching firsts. I check out some books and plan to start looking through them tonight while listening to the game. The Giants are playing the Dodgers, and Drysdale's going for number five. When I get home, there's a note on the door.

Irrigation's coming in. Meet me at the school. I'll be there at 5:00. Bring a towel.

Kel

I'm late. It's a quarter after when I hop on my ten-speed.

The traffic at Glendale sets up perfectly, and I zip through the crosswalk without dismounting. I head up Fifth Street and take the rise at full speed. Where the asphalt ends, my bike veers around the concrete irrigation stand with its large red wheel at the top and the water already churning and echoing deep inside, and then I coast down the dirt path between redwood fences, splashing through a little stream from someone's over-flowing backyard. I clatter past "the big tree," where my friend Ed does most of his fighting, and on to where the asphalt picks up again behind the school.

The water covers the bottom four inches of the fences on the Major and Senior fields. Along the foul lines, it's shallower. By tomorrow afternoon it will be soaked in.

Kelly's walking through a stretch in her bare feet. It's only about an inch deep. She's reaching down and flipping stuff off to the side. She sees me coming and yells out, "Willie, where ya been?"

"Library."

She shakes her head and goes back to work.

I weave my bike through the gate and lay it down next to her flip-flops. "Aren't you wearing shoes for this?"

"Nope. Don't need 'em."

"Where's your towel?"

"You brought one."

I look down at my old Converse shoes sticking out below my jeans, decide to keep them on, and then look around.

Across the Majors' infield, two boys are raising rooster tails with their bikes. They jump the berm and then stop with a brodie on the sidewalk by the bike racks.

"We're about the only ones here," I say.

"Yeah, after your speech, they all left for the big leagues."

"Hey, Mr. Estes liked it. Your dad...he loved it."

"Nah, it was good, Willie."

I fall in line behind her, looking for anything that might end our season. Kelly's wearing blue-jean cutoffs and a yellow T-shirt that's hard to look at in the sun. Her legs are more tan than mine. She's always tan. Her mother's the same way. Maybe it's all the camping, hiking, and sailing they do.

I ask, "How'd you get over here?" She keeps toeing at the grass below the water with her bare feet; doesn't look up. "Brenda dropped me off. We went shopping for bathing suits."

"You leave on Tuesday?"

"Yeah."

"How many games you going to miss?"

"Just two."

"You want to come over and listen to the Dodgers tonight? Drysdale's up again."

"Can't. My dad's taking us to a movie. He's not working tonight." She reaches down and picks up a pop-top, examines it. "I have to be home by 6:30. Oh, I almost forgot. I've got a first for your list. My dad told me." She turns in my direction and says the next thing like she's picturing the words in her head: "First player chosen in Major League Baseball's first amateur draft."

"I don't know. Babe Ruth?"

"Rick Monday. In 1965. It's kind of trick question. They didn't start drafting players until three years ago."

"Nice one."

She tosses the pop-top aside and asks, "You know what time it is?" I start to check my Timex, and then she's by me, running at full speed, water flying off her heels, the most athletic legs I've ever seen. My legs are like sticks. Her arms rise to the sky and she leans back. As if cushioned by invisible hands, her butt settles onto the sloppy grass, and then she glides, left leg straight, skimming the surface, right leg tucked, bent at the knee. It's a beautiful sight. She slides and slides, and as she slows, she plants the heel of her left foot, pops up and spins to face me. She's not even breathing heavy when she yells back, "Time to play ball!"

She teaches me how to slide, one leg up, the other bent, just like she did it, just like her dad taught her. He also taught her the pop-up slide, the fadeaway, and the hook — versions for later. Today, she says, we're sticking with the fundamentals, and by the end of our session, I'm sliding as smooth as a goose. We have a contest to see who can slide the farthest with the loser buying the winner a Mountain Dew. She wins. That's nothing new. But sliding without killing myself is a first.

We're soaked when we're done, and you can see the outline of her bra under her shirt. That kind of thing is no big deal to her. If she wasn't Kelly, it might be a bigger deal to me. We share my towel to dry off. I give her a ride on my bike, but she pedals, and I straddle the rear tire while sitting on the book rack. Later that night, Drysdale beats the Giants three-nothing. Now he's only one shy of a first.

Little League resumes Monday night. I don't have a game, but Kelly's playing. I'm eating a bullet pop, the only eighth grade boy watching girls' softball, except for Ed Guerin. He's straddling his Sting-Ray at the edge of the stands. I hear he's going steady with Mary Anne Lempky now. She plays for the

Quails — their pitcher — and she is a girl of legendary status in my grade. Mary Anne's an early bloomer — Ed says she's stacked — and I can confirm from having PE the same hour as Ed that he's way ahead of most of us as well. There's a rumor he's actually fifteen. Ed's eyes are on Mary Anne and his mind is on baseball. He's rounding the bases. I can tell.

This particular field doesn't have a fence. A ball hit to left field will hit the Seniors' fence to the north, and one hit to right field will hit the Majors' fence to the east. But the fences arc toward each other in center field and never touch, creating a gap that runs deep into the dark. Kelly's on the Hawks and is three for three so far. It's a joke. She's so much better than the other girls. In Kelly's next time up, Mary Anne's face stops a line drive that would have shot the gap. Her glove never moves. She drops like a bag of bats. Coaches and parents crash the field, including Dr. Barrett and Mary Anne's dad, a big guy with a bald head and a large gut.

Eventually, Mr. Lempky carries poor sobbing Mary Anne off the field while we applaud. She's got a bag of ice on her mouth and blood splattered across the QUAILS on her chest. Kelly's standing on first, silent and still, like I only saw her once before when we found the dead dog. Her dad goes over and puts both hands on her shoulders. Bent at the waist, he's saying something, while she wipes her eyes and stares at the huddle of people around Mary Anne, sitting in the first row of the bleachers. Then he squats down, looks up at Kelly, and pats her on the hip, talking the whole time. The ump signals *play ball*. Her dad stands, but before he backs away, he pulls her cap down over her face.

When she pulls it up, she's smiling. She claps twice and takes her stance at first, left foot on the bag, hands on knees. Then she rises up and claps twice more. He said something. Maybe something from my speech or from Mr. Estes' list, like *Mary Anne was caught off base,* or something else that will line up with *fundamentals* and *playing to your strength* the next time she's showing me how to charge a grounder or tag a runner sliding into second. Whatever it was, she's back.

After the game, I tell her Mary Anne's lip was cut; they took her to get stitches, but that she'll be okay. We talk a bit about her trip to Mexico and that it's too bad she'll miss Drysdale's shot at the record and my game tomorrow, all on the same night. She reminds me, "Use your stance," and demonstrates it while holding a rainbow snow-cone in one hand and her glove in the other. Her dad calls out and waves from his car.

"I gotta go," she says. "Remember to lean back going into your slide. We'll do some batting practice when I get back." She's running backwards now, toward the dark of the parking lot. "See you next week."

Playing ball, swimming, or losing Mountain Dew bets at ping-pong, I've spent parts of almost every week of every summer since third grade in Kelly Barrett's backyard. Now, the summer's over, and I haven't talked to Kel since the night she pasted Mary Anne's mouth with a line drive back in June. High school starts this morning. The moms have worked out a carpool, and I'm sitting on a boulder out by our front walkway. Mrs. Barrett will be by soon. I can hear the traffic on Glendale — all the dads going back to work after Labor Day. A kid from up the street peddles past on his way to the grade school. It looks and sounds like a normal day. Even the Giants are in second place once again behind the Cardinals. But things sure don't feel normal.

Kelly's dad was killed in a plane crash the Saturday after they left for Mexico. I was listening to the Dodgers' game when my parents told me. Drysdale's streak ended that same night. As a matter of fact, just four days before, Drysdale set the record with his sixth shutout. This was on the same night Bobby Kennedy was shot. It was a weird week. My parents said that Dr. Barrett was helping a woman who'd broken both her legs in a dune buggy accident. He offered to ride with her in a private plane to a hospital. It had just taken off, and only seconds later it crashed. Kelly and her mom saw it happen. Her sisters were somewhere else. That's all I know.

My mom did a lot of crying and kept saying *tragic* over and over during the days before the funeral. She said I didn't have to go. But I kind of wanted to. I was sad in a way that was different from when I saw the dog a couple years ago, or when Kennedy died earlier in the week. There was more to it. Sure, I felt sad for Dr. Barrett, and a little sad for myself. But I was more sad for Kelly. I wanted to see her, but at the same time I wasn't sure what to say.

When I did see her, she wore a black dress. As she walked into the church, her face was blank. I sat a few rows behind her with my parents and stared at her brown hair through the whole service. Things were said. People cried. Music played. When she walked away at the end, she was holding Mrs. Barrett's hand. She looked at me and didn't smile. It was like the look she had standing on first a couple weeks before, only now, her eyes seemed empty. That's how the whole day felt — empty. I wanted to say something, maybe "sorry." I don't know, is that enough? What do you say? Mostly I wanted to touch her. That sounds weird. Hold her hand, maybe, or just dance like we did at Junior Assembly and talk about baseball.

We went over to their house afterwards. They had food. Mrs. Barrett hugged me when I came in, pulled me right into her chest and kissed my forehead. She leaned back and cupped my chin like she'd done a few weeks earlier and said, "It's going to be all right. Everything's going to be all right." She pulled me back to her while my parents closed the circle. They were all crying except me, and I thought maybe I should be, too.

My mom asked about the girls. I could see Brenda and Julie talking in the living room with people I didn't know. "Kelly's not doing well," Mrs. Barrett said. "She's in her room. I think I'll just leave her alone for now."

That was it. She wanted to be alone. I ate some chocolate-covered strawberries, grabbed a Dew, then moved to the Arcadia door. Drysdale, tail wagging, was standing at the glass with a baseball in his mouth. The yard was cleaned up and the boat was gone. I went outside and threw him grounders for a while, and then just sat until my mom called me in to leave. Kelly, Brenda, Julie, and their mom went to California for the rest of the summer. They took Drysdale and stayed with Mrs. Barrett's sister in Van Nuys. I watered their plants and mowed the grass while they were gone. Every two weeks, Mrs. Barrett sent me a check for ten dollars.

The Little League season ended before the Fourth of July. Moose and Peter knocked the snot out of the ball and were all-stars again. With Mary Anne around, Ed had trouble focusing. His hitting suffered, but behind the plate he could talk a batter into an out. The rest of the summer was like playing in a game when you're down by ten runs. It felt hopeless and went on forever. I hung out with Moose and Peter some until family vacations broke that up. I listened to the Giants when they played the Dodgers, and I worked on my list.

It was sure strange not seeing Kelly in the stands during the season. I got a ton of walks using her stance.

Any time I got on base and second was open, I took it, and sometimes third base as well. The catchers only threw me out twice. Getting the sliding down made all the difference. I worked on it when irrigation came in at the school, the park, or a nearby church. Sometimes, I got Ed to meet me with his minibike whenever he wasn't trying to cop a feel at Mary Anne's house.

I had discovered something. What worked best for me was not *thinking* about fundamentals; it was *seeing* the fundamentals — remembering how Kelly looked gliding through the wet grass. I'd just picture her leaning back, arms rising, right leg tucking as she settled into her slide. Then I'd start running, pick out a spot ahead of me, and let it happen. It worked. I might even be able to beat her in a distance contest now. So, we won the pennant, I was second in the league in stolen bases, and Kelly missed it all. Those were firsts for me. It was a summer of firsts.

I stand when I hear the Barrett's old Mercedes coming down the street to pick me up. The smell of the diesel reminds me of trips to the batting cage with Kelly and her dad. Kelly has only been back from California for a week. Now it's just her and her mom at their house since Julie and Brenda have started up at ASU. According to my mom, Kel's still in a slump. If she was dropping her elbow or stepping in the bucket (two things she had said

I was doing), maybe I could help. I probably should have gone over to her house to see her like my mom wanted. But I didn't know what to say. I still don't. What if she'd started to cry? What was I supposed to do, sit there like a dork while she ran off somewhere and I had to explain to Mrs. Barrett it wasn't my fault?

Kelly's riding shotgun when I get in the backseat. Jill and her twin brother Geoffrey scoot over to make room. Mrs. Barrett looks over her shoulder. I'm behind her. "Good morning, Charlie. I haven't seen you in a while."

The twins look at me and we all nod. "Morning."

Kelly's mom pulls onto Glendale. "Everyone ready for your first day?"

No one speaks up, so I say, "I hope so."

"Well, you'll do just fine." She pauses for a second. "I hope everyone's going to the dance on Friday."

No one steps to the plate on that one either. Last week, a notice came in the mail for the parents.

"Charlie," Kelly's mom says, "you be sure to dance with Kelly. I remember what a good team you two made at Junior Assembly."

Jill whispers something to Geoffrey that I can't hear.

Mrs. Barrett turns right at Central Avenue and comes to a stoplight a little ways down.

"By the way, Charlie," she says, "You did a great job with the yard. I never had a chance to thank you. Your mom said the mower gave you trouble. Did it?"

"Just one time. It turned out to be the spark plug."

"Listen to you. Your voice is starting to sound just like your dad's."

I suppose it was, but when Mrs. Barrett said "dad," my stomach flinched the way it does when a pitch comes in too close. I look over at Kelly. She's staring out the window. Mrs. Barrett turns up the radio. Nobody talks for much of the way. Geoffrey and Jill are still whispering things I can't hear.

At a break in the music, "Chopper Dave" says there are no accidents to report and wishes all the parents a happy first day of school. The news guy says something about Nixon leading Humphrey in a poll and that we'll break one hundred degrees again. The sports guy says the Giants tied the Cubs in the second game of a double-header yesterday. Tied. Their first game to end in a tie this season.

"Looks like your Giants are putting up a fight." Mrs. Barrett is looking at me in the rearview mirror. "Kelly's Dodgers aren't in such good shape."

"They're not the same team without Wills." I'm thinking that might help, but Kelly doesn't look back, doesn't move at all. Then I add, "How's Drysdale?"

Mrs. Barrett looks at Kelly and asks, "How would you say he is, Kelly?"

She looks at her mom, then over her shoulder at me for a second. "Fine, I guess."

"Oh, you know Drysdale," Mrs. Barrett says. "He's still trotting around the yard with that ball in his mouth.

We sold the boat, you know. Ole Drysdale's out there sniffing around where it used to be. I think he misses laying in the shade of that thing." Her voice gets high at the end. In the mirror I can see she's blinking hard. She clears her throat. "I noticed the grass came back." She checks over her shoulder to change lanes and gives me a weak smile. I'm thinking, *yes, let's talk about the grass.* I go into some detail about my watering schedule, how the grass began to fill in after I gave it a little extra hose time every other day, how my goal had been to get it as thick and green as the outfield at Candlestick Park. I talk more than I ever do with an adult, and I'm not sure if anyone in the car is even listening, but it makes the drive to school feel almost normal.

At the school, the twins are off to their lockers before Mrs. Barrett gets out of the car. I could go, but I hang back by the trunk to wait for Kelly. Mrs. Barrett meets up with her as she comes around the front. Kelly's wearing a skirt; a sure sign that summer is over. Her hair is longer now and tied in a ponytail. Mrs. Barrett ruffles Kelly's shoulders — the coach trying to cheer her team on. *It's not over until the last out is made.* It just pops into my head. I don't remember that one from Mr. Estes' list; much of that list has faded. Maybe I could use it on Kelly, but it doesn't exactly fit. Still, it seems like something her dad would have said.

Mrs. Barrett is stroking Kelly's hair now, while saying something. Kelly smiles briefly. Mrs. Barrett kisses her on the cheek and then nudges her in my direction. We walk under the big Central High sign for the first time as freshman. She doesn't ask me about the Giants, or about my season, or about Don Drysdale's record. She doesn't ask me anything. It feels like it does when I haven't seen my cousins in a while — I have to get to know them all over again. I ask her what she has for first period. She says, "English." I say, "Me, too." We have the same Algebra class as well. When I break off to my locker, I say, "Bye, Kel," and she says, "Bye, Charlie," Not *Bye, Willie.* It's like she's not even trying.

Other than English and Algebra, I hardly see her; we even have different lunch hours. Mrs. Barrett does most of the talking during the carpool the rest of the week, and she reminds me again on Friday morning to be sure to dance with Kelly. Friday night, my mom drops Peter, Moose, and me off at the school. The principal calls the event a "freshman mixer," a way for all the ninth graders coming in from different schools to get to know each other. The flyer said: *Gentlemen will wear ties.* We're gentlemen now, but Moose, I mean Randy — he's on a kick to use his real name, and he's wearing contacts — thinks we look like a bunch of rejects: short sleeve shirts, dress pants, and wingtips. I'm actually wearing penny loafers, but according to Randy, I'm still a pud because I have a clip-on tie.

The principal greets us at the double doors of the gym. A lot of kids are already here. He shakes our hands, passes us to the vice-principal, and we shake hers. Osgood, the first baseman on my team, is ahead of us in line. I haven't seen him since the season ended, not even this week. The school's big. "Long time, no see," he says and shakes my hand. That's the way it goes, I guess. We're gentlemen now, and gentlemen shake hands. So, we move around, extending our hands to people we haven't seen in three months, some of them, like me, an inch or so taller since graduation in June. That was the last time most of us guys wore a tie, although I did have one on at Dr. Barrett's funeral.

Tonight, only about half of the lights in the gym are turned on. Streamers, balloons, and a disc jockey blasting music from a platform set up under a raised basketball hoop have turned this place into a dance. Some of the balloons are tumbling on the floor, but most are still in bunches attached to long tables brought over from the cafeteria. The DJ is playing "Satisfaction," and quite a few guys are dancing. They're the ones with girlfriends: guys who are pretty good dancers, or think they are pretty good dancers. I'm not any of those.

Ed Guerin's in the corner with a guy I don't know. Ed's pointing over to a group of girls huddled at a nearby table. When he sees me, he smiles, and I notice something kind of shiny in his mouth. He motions to come over. I work my way through the non-dancers. Ed sticks out his hand. I shake it and start to laugh.

"What?" he says.

"Nothing," I say. All of a sudden, Ed's a gentleman, too.

"This is Joe," Ed says. "He went to Orangewood."

Joe just nods: he knows who he is.

"Joe's folks are out of town," Ed says. "We're going over later and getting blitzed. Rusty's got some Colt 45 he's gonna sell me. We're thinking of asking those girls."

He points to the table. "The one with her back to us keeps looking over her shoulder, pretending she doesn't see us. And look at that other one. I've already danced with her. She's a fox." Ed has a focus now that he never had at the plate. He looks at me and says, "What do you think? You want to come over?"

"No, I don't think so."

"Oh, come on, don't be a candy-ass."

He's waiting for an excuse, and I can't come up with one except maybe that I have to babysit my little sister — a real candy-ass excuse — so l just change the subject. I lift my chin toward him. "What's with the tooth?"

"It's a cap. Solid silver. Boss, huh. Mary Anne's dad popped me."

"He knocked out your tooth?"

"No, he didn't actually slug me. He kind of pushed me. I broke the tooth on a rock."

"Ed, what are you talking about?" Joe must know a story's coming that he's already heard. He slaps Ed on the shoulder and walks away.

Ed calls out, "Meet me in the parking lot at nine."

When he looks back at me, it takes a second before he finds his place again. "Well, we — Mary Anne and me — we're making out in her backyard about three weeks ago. Wow, I haven't seen you since then. You know her mouth's all healed up. We're lying in the grass in her backyard, out on the side where the fence connects with the house. No one can see us. There's a full moon. It's kind of romantic, and we're getting pretty heavy. We thought her dad was asleep. I guess he was, but I don't know why he came outside to the backyard. Anyway, we're next to the big air conditioner. Those things make a ton of noise. Mary Anne has on this tank top...no bra. You wouldn't believe the jugs on her. So, I'm safe at second, feeling her up...you know, really working her."

Ed's got his hands and arms into the story now. He looks like he's rinsing his jersey in the sink.

He goes on. "I'm thinking about trying for third. So, I make a joke about it being hot outside and then start pulling her top over her head. She kind of giggles, and pulls it back down, so I pop the snap on her cutoffs and go for the zipper. Next thing I know, I'm flying through the air. Land on my face. I swear to God, at that moment, I thought of your nose. Turns out it was fine. Chipped half my front tooth, though, and my lip swelled. Well, when I look up, her dad's lifting Mary Anne off the ground. She might have screamed when he first grabbed me, I'm not sure, but now she's crying her guts out. He starts to walk her toward the patio, but she takes off for the back door without him. That's when he turns. He just stands there for a second. All he's got on is an undershirt, boxers, and some slippers. He points a big hairy arm at me. I can see his hand shaking. Man, I figure he's gonna freak out, but all he says, real calm like, is 'Stay away from my girl.' Nothing else. Then he goes inside. Kind of funny, huh?"

It takes a moment, then I ask, "What about Mary Anne? Is she here?"

"No way. She's grounded till the day after next year. I won't be seeing her anymore."

I'm ready to move on. Ed, too. He says he's going to scarf down a few of those mini tacos, then head over to the table of girls.

"I see Kelly's back," he says.

"Yeah, about two weeks ago."

"No, dipshit, I mean I saw her leave the gym before you came over." He points over to where about fifty people are dancing now. "She must have been taking a whiz." Ed heads for the tacos.

Kelly's dancing a fast dance. According to the DJ, it's "Love Me Two Times" by The Doors. She's with someone I recognize from Algebra, but I don't know his name. She's wearing a dress without sleeves, and even in this dim light she looks tan. Every so often, the guy she's dancing with shouts something in her direction, and she smiles for a moment. Heads are bobbing, blocking my view, so I keep shifting. She sees me and gives a casual wave. There's a look on her face, like a question. It's not the dazed look she gave me at the funeral, but it pulls at me just the same, from deep under my ribs. It's hard to explain. I want to dance with her.

When the song finishes, she heads towards a table where Jill is sitting, drinking something out of a Styrofoam cup. Jill's craning her neck toward the dancers. The disk jockey says, "Let's see if we can't get everyone out here...this is Simon and Garfunkel... 'Scarborough Fair.'"

I reach the table before she sits down. "Kel." She turns, and for the first time I notice that we're about the same height. She's also wearing makeup on her eyes.

"Charlie."

"I promised your mom I'd ask you to dance." It sounds wrong after I say it.

She looks at Jill, and Jill's looking at me over the top of her cup.

"No, I mean she said we should dance. So, do you want to dance?"

"Sure."

It's a slow song, and the DJ gets his way — most everyone goes out there. It's not the kind of dancing you train for. There are no fundamentals to it. The couples are clutching, making their own tight little circles, and there's not a lot of talking; mostly thinking. I take Kelly's right hand in my left and place my other hand against her back, below her shoulder blades. There's enough space between us for a volleyball and a conversation. Maybe we can just talk about baseball.

Before we start, I ask, "Do you want to do the waltz or the fox trot?" I smile to let her know it was a joke.

She looks at the dancers around us, then back to me. "How about neither." We maintain our Junior Assembly position and begin swaying back and forth through our own circle, looking past each other. She doesn't talk, but the dancing sort of softens things, like how massaging the leather works the stiffness out of a new glove. Simon and Garfunkel are starting the second verse before I decide what to say next.

"See if you can answer this."

"Okay."

I lob one in. "When was the first indoor All-Star Game played, and where?"

She answers right away. "That was two months ago in the Astrodome."

"Very good. You lead one nothing. You want another?"

"Sure."

"Who was the first major league pitcher to throw six shutouts in a row?"

"My uncle told me Drysdale got it."

"Right again. That's two nothing...You know, it's on my list."

"So, you're still working on it."

"I have to. Got to write a book someday."

"How many do you have so far?"

"Fifty-three."

She looks at me. "Fifty-three! Sounds like you've got plenty for a book."

"No, I need a bunch more. Besides, I'm waiting to add you."

She scrunches her eyebrows.

"The first girl to play major league baseball," I say. "Kelly Elizabeth Barrett — shortstop for the Los Angeles Dodgers, nineteen...what would that be...nineteen seventy-six? That'll give you four years in the minors after high school before they call you up."

"I'm not going to college?"

"You're right. After college. You'll go from the College World Series to Dodger Stadium and become the first rookie since Maury Wills to lead the league in stolen bases."

She's quiet and looks away.

I wonder if she's thinking of the picture in her hallway of Wills and her dad. I hope I haven't ruined things.

She says, "I've got one for you."

"One what?"

"For your list." I can tell she's putting something together in her head. "Who's the first player to hit a grand slam home run in his first at-bat this century?"

The question stuns me. She's smiling that gap-toothed smile. She knows I know. It happened on my birthday while she was away. I say, "I've already added it. Bobby Bonds, San Francisco Giants. June 25, 1968, in the sixth inning against the Los Angeles Dodgers."

It's like a gift, and there's a warmth swelling in my throat. Any normal summer, she would have been at my house eating birthday cake and listening to the game live on the radio.

"Who told you?" It's a stupid question, but it's all I can get out.

"I saw it on TV when we were in California. My uncle watches all the games."

We go back to looking past each other, but now we're dancing closer together as Simon and Garfunkel finish. Things are feeling almost normal. The DJ says, "I want everyone to stay out there. Let's turn the lights down low for this one. One of my favorites, and a tune that will mean more as you get older...'Yesterday.'"

I don't even ask her. We just start dancing again.

She says, "How'd your season go?"

"Pretty good. We won the pennant."

"That's more than pretty good. How'd you do?"

"More walks than strikeouts."

"The stance worked, huh?"

"Helfinstine didn't want me to use it at first. He thought it looked crazy."

"Of course, it looks crazy. Part of it is to bug the pitcher."

"He got used to it. Between the walks and the bunts, I was on base so much he moved me up to lead-off."

"Wow, so how'd the stealing go?"

"I did just what you said. Get a good lead. Weight on my toes. Stay relaxed — "

She kind of shakes me. "No, I mean, how many bases did you steal?"

I look at her and smile. "I didn't lead the league, but I came in second."

She stops and pulls back long enough to say, "Willie, that's great!" Then we start circling again. "I told you. See how it works. It's all about fundamentals, playing to your strengths. My dad says if — "

She squeezes my hand and stares past my shoulder. I look straight ahead as well. We go a full rotation, then a second, without saying a word. Maybe there's nothing I need to say. The song will end. Some other song will begin, something faster, and I'll walk her back to where Jill is sitting, so I don't have to dance and look like a clod. We'll talk a little more: new teachers, new friends, and if we talk about last summer, or next summer, we'll talk about baseball. Maybe we'll share some punch. The guy from Algebra will ask her to dance again. When the mixer has mixed us up enough, we'll head home. Tomorrow, we'll all wake up surprised and happy that it's Saturday, and Ed's girl, Mary Anne, won't even know what she missed. She'll probably still be grounded, still be mad at her dad, the same hairy-armed guy I saw carry her off the field on the last normal night of the summer. Kelly looked dazed that night, standing on first base. Then Dr. Barrett patted her on the hip and whispered something that brought her back. Something fundamental. I can picture him talking to her.

We're still circling, silently. I feel like I do in that dream, where I'm rounding the bases and never touch the bags. It should be the easiest thing. "Kel, I'm sorry. I know you miss him."

I feel her relax, and for a second, I think she's going to faint. She lets go of my left hand and puts both her arms around my neck. She rests her forehead on my shoulder, like we're going steady. Then her breathing changes to small quiet tugs. She's crying. Our little patch of hardwood floor circles below us. My heart's beating like it does when I'm leading off first and the pitcher has come set, the way it beats in that moment before I'll either be racing to second or diving back to the bag.

Kelly tilts her face into my neck. I can feel her breath, then her voice, soft and tired. "I miss him so much.... Thank you, Charlie." She says this like I had just found something of hers she thought was lost forever.

I say, "You're welcome." It sounds polite but not entirely right. I do know that holding her feels right. It feels sad and it feels warm, all at the same time. After a few more turns, I realize that the music has changed. The couples around us are moving to a faster rhythm. We stop, then break our hold on one another. Kelly has a tissue, and she wipes her eyes.

I take her hand and lead her out the double doors before anyone can ask. The night is warm. We walk along the side of the gym, then across the tennis courts. It's dark except for the lights of the city outside the school grounds. We're not saying anything; just walking, holding hands, trying to figure things out. The thought of kissing her doesn't seem as far out in left anymore. A cool breeze drifts off the baseball fields just ahead of us. They're flooded. The water's still coming in. I can hear it bubbling, and the sound gets louder as we move farther from the gym and the music.

"You know what time it is?" I say. I motion out to the fields.

We leave our shoes on the tennis court, and we run. When my bare feet first touch the water, Kelly's not far behind, charging hard. She yells, "I don't have a towel." It sounds strange coming from her. It's not normal. None of this is normal. It's all new. I pull off my clip-on tie and throw it over my shoulder. Kelly's laughing, splashing through the water; she hasn't passed me yet.

She calls out, "I'll bet you a Dew."

I pick a spot just ahead where some leaves float over a ripple. In my mind I can see her from three months ago: leaning back, arms rising to the sky, the gentle land-ing...sliding, sliding, gliding.

WHO WE WERE AT TWELVE

My friend Benjamin and I were spies. We were sixth-graders in 1964, and for the first three months of that year, he was the station chief, and I was his protégé in our two-man neighborhood spy ring. On weekends we scaled redwood fences, hid behind oleander and juniper hedges, air conditioner compressors, and above-ground swimming pools. We perched on sturdy branches deep within the canopy of our neighbors' orange and grapefruit trees, consuming the pilfered fruit until our tongues and saliva thickened and we could unload a loogie like an eighth grader. We were the repository of Linger Lane's backyard secrets. Those were careless days.

Benjamin coined our last mission "Operation Domino." It was an elaborate two-phase plan, which I suspected he'd been designing for some time. Friday, the

first night of Easter Break, I knocked on the door at Headquarters, his bedroom.

"Albert," he said.

"Einstein," I responded.

He cracked the door. After allowing me in the dark-
ened room, he retrieved the spiral-bound *Top Top Secret*
notebook from behind the *Encyclopedia Britannicas*.
Benjamin laid the notebook open under the light of his
goose-neck lamp. Across two pages he'd drawn a
schematic: his backyard, the Andersons', and the Ciprianos', all in a row, with fences and alley behind. I knew
immediately this was about revenge on Adam Cipriano, a
classmate and the only other sixth grader on the block.

I'd met Adam near the end of Christmas break, a couple
days after my family moved from a downtown apartment
near the Phoenix hospital where my father worked. It was
our first house, but my second school that year. My
mother pried me away from afternoon reruns and sent
me to the curb with a can of black paint, a brush, some
stencils, and her hope: "You just might make a new friend
while you do this."

That's what I was afraid of — making friends — something that had not been easy for me. I was eleven, small
boned, with my mother's narrow, angelic face, and quiet.
In a week, I'd be the new kid again.

Except for the four-foot-high wagon wheel bordering the small porch, our house was identical to the other single-level, asphalt-tiled, brick boxes on the street. The houses even had the same floor plan. I laid the stencils on the curb in the order my mother had prescribed — 4-6-2-6 — and staked our claim with zeal, aligning and realigning. I wanted the number perfect. Adam peddled over on his new, black Sting-Ray. Of course, I didn't know who he was then. He was just a kid with dark, wide-set eyes and eyebrows seemingly cut from black construction paper and pasted to his forehead. His bike made a rat-ta-tat sound from cards he'd clothes-pinned to the fork, something I liked to do. *Remember, you can stop the world with that smile of yours*, I heard my mother say. I smiled from my crouched position and Adam stopped. But before he spoke, I sensed trouble — he'd used perfectly good baseball trading cards. Now they were ruined. He straddled the crossbar and said, "What's your name?" emphasizing *your*.

I stood and rubbed my palms on my jeans, resisting the urge to run. "Rick," I said. It sounded like an apology. "What's your name?" I took a step back from this boy no taller than me but twice my girth. His ankles were thick as salamis.

He sighted through the viewfinder of a Kodak Instamatic, which was looped around his wrist. "Puddin' Tain," he said. "Ask me again and I'll tell you the same." He laughed and took a photograph of my stricken face.

Then, mouthing sound effects, he gunned his handlebar throttle and attempted a pathetic wheelie over the curb. His effort smudged my freshly painted numbers, causing him to laugh even louder as he circled me a few times before charging across the street to his house, where he dismounted in one motion, allowing his bike to crash into the carport.

I ran inside.

"Oh, I'm sure it's not that bad," my mother said while scrubbing the sink. "Let's clear this up. Shall we?"

In a few minutes, we stood on the Ciprianos' porch, my mother in her Capri pants, my baby brother babbling on her hip, my kid sister and me silent behind her. My mother spoke at some length in the same diplomatic voice I would intone to my advantage in later years. She spoke of boys being boys and getting off on the wrong foot and how Adam probably didn't realize he'd smudged my impeccable, curbside artwork. But Mrs. C stiffened. She pulled Adam securely to her side and said she didn't appreciate her angel being accused of something he said he didn't do. And my mother bristled at the suggestion that her son was the liar in this affair. "He's never, ever lied to me," she said. And that was the truth. I depended on my parents' adoration to bolster my shaky confidence. Mrs. Cipriano concluded with a brief sermon, capping it with the phrase *our Lord in Heaven shall be our judge,* and slammed the door in our faces.

My mother dragged us back to our house in a quick-paced huff. She leaned against the kitchen sink and folded her arms. "That boy's going to be trouble," she said. "And that mother! Oh!" She turned the faucet on and roughed up a bar of soap. "I've known boys like him. He won't change. It's like I've always said, 'Who you are at twelve is who you're going to be.'" She stomped her foot, turned, and, while scrubbing her hands, said, "You are never to play with that boy. Understand? You are never to enter that house." She didn't wait for my affirmation. We both knew I wouldn't disobey. I went back outside so my mother could slam kitchen cupboards in private.

I was feeling pretty low. Not only had I not made any friends, I had an enemy. And I'd never heard her maxim — *who you are at twelve is who you're going to be.* It jarred my literal mind. I'd be twelve in less than a year. I was still an inch shy of five feet. I couldn't throw a curve ball or ride a unicycle. The thought of forever being stuck with these deficiencies spurred me to inaction. I sat on the curb.

It was then that Benjamin ambled from the shadow of an orange tree in his front yard and sat by me. He was a head-and-a-half taller and thin as a pencil. "Don't worry about Wheezy," he said. "He got me with that Puddin' Tain routine, too."

"Wheezy?"

"Adam. He's got asthma. Thinks it's a secret, but I've seen him use his inhaler." Benjamin looked toward Adam's house. "He must have gotten the camera for

Christmas. I like it. I'm surprised the ignoramus figured out how to use it."

He looked me over, while I basked in what felt like a safe zone. "Rick what?" he asked.

"Huh?"

"Your last name?"

"Zwieback."

"Anybody ever call you Swayback?"

"Yeah," I said, lowering my head.

"That won't do. I'll come up with something."

The street was quiet except for the doves cooing in the citrus trees. Benjamin surveyed the neighborhood, filling me in on names and occupations. (He already knew my father was a doctor.) Across the street, Mrs. Grant — code name *Fudgesicle Lady* — lived alone with her dachshund Patsy on one side of Benjamin. On the other side were the Andersons, then the Ciprianos. Both Mr. and Mrs. Anderson delivered the mail. Their seventeen-year-old daughter Amy was going steady with Tony Cipriano, Adam's fifteen-year-old brother. Both were in high school.

"See the Anderson's mailbox?" Benjamin said.

I looked across the street. "No."

"That's because it's not there," he said. "Tony annihilated it with his mom's Beetle. Showing off for Amy." He pursed his lips and shook his head. "Ironic, isn't it."

"Yes," I said, although I had no idea what he was talking about, much less what "ironic" meant.

He pointed to the house next to the Andersons'. "Of course, that's where the Ciprianos live. They're trouble."

"That's what my mom says."

"I've had them under surveillance. You ever spy before?"

I hadn't, so Benjamin coached me. We spent hours crouched behind fences, and he taught me to shift my weight so my feet didn't fall asleep in case we had to run. When I ate oranges, I threw the rinds into the giant oleanders behind the alley — *leave no trace.* Often, our missions began by crawling through Mrs. Grant's dog door and taking a fudgesicle from her freezer. "We live off the land," Benjamin said. "We appropriate when we have to." He told me I'd see some amazing things, and he was right — like the father who boiled dead chickens to make vertebrae necklaces for his Indian Princess tribe or Mrs. Grant's dachshund Patsy who ate a whole ham and then threw it up. Benjamin cataloged the intelligence in the *Top Top Secret* notebook. But nothing could beat spying on Tony and Amy when they made out. Amy was a blonde with vanilla skin. She'd tap the horn of her Fairlane and wave as Benjamin and I walked to the bus stop in the morning. I'd smile and wave back. Once, when it rained, she gave us a lift down the street. She smelled like baby powder.

The times her parents were out, Tony hopped the fence with the exuberance of a jungle cat. Fully clothed, he and Amy writhed on a beach towel in her backyard or on the couch in the family room, their lips rarely parting as Tony's hands explored her chest. Fortunately, she never closed the curtains across the sliding glass doors. It was a scene more explicit than anything on TV. What Tony and Amy did was the kind of hard-core action James Bond was up to in the theaters, or so I imagined.

To Benjamin there were two enemies in the world, the Soviet Union and Adam Cipriano. I was never as concerned with Russian spies, but in Adam we had a common loathing. That was about all we had in common. Every week Benjamin checked out books from the library and actually read them — *The Hobbit, Kidnapped, Animal Farm,* and many others. He read them leaning against the backstop while I played tetherball or swung from the metal rings at recess. Blue ribbons from past science fair projects were tacked to his corkboard, and a lighted globe sat on his desk. He used words like *appropriate, surveillance,* and *ignoramus* — gargantuan words that set my skin buzzing with their capacity to simultaneously impress and confuse. On many weekend nights, I lay in a near trance on his bed as he drew long, ominous groans across his cello and recounted wild tales of his father working for the CIA and kidnappings in Prague. Growing in his refrigerator was a super-secret bacteria destined for Khrushchev's orange juice. He was clearly the smartest kid in sixth grade, if not the whole school. And he was my best friend.

He started calling me "Watson," a reference to Sherlock Holmes's companion, but it didn't take at school. Adam dubbed me "Midge," short for Midget. I figured Midge was better than Wheezy and not any worse than Gimp, Cross-eyes, Dumbo, Bugs, or Stick. And it was far better than "Rat." That's what Adam called Benjamin. He wasn't a snitch. It was the particular way he looked in the class picture on Mrs. Oldmeyer's bulletin board. I noticed it my first day of class. In the photo (taken before I arrived) Benjamin's nose and mouth protruded, and he looked skittish. Not so much like a rat, but more like a turtle who'd lost his shell: a long neck and narrow sloping shoulders. He was shaped like a boy who peered through fences.

About the second week of January, the class photo disappeared. Presumably stolen. Mrs. Oldmeyer was aghast that a sixth-grade thief resided in our midst. She pointed a jiggly arm at the empty space on the bulletin board and laid down some heavy shame on the perpetrator, claiming that Lee Harvey Oswald had been a thief as a child and look where it got him. Even though she loitered around Adam's desk, I was sure it was Benjamin who'd stolen that photograph. He hated it. But I was wrong. The next day, it was back on display. The thief had drawn whiskers under Benjamin's nose and an impressive wedge of cheese near his mouth. Two tiny rat hands with spiny fingers grasped the cheese. A blue caption read *Mmmm good.*

Later, at the far end of our lunch table, Gimp, Stevie,

and Bugs laughed while Adam put on a show. He held his Sloppy Joe to his mouth, took small, rapid bites, and extended his neck, glancing from side to side as if a predator lurked. "Mmmm, good," he said.

Benjamin's eyes seemed to glisten, and I was afraid he might cry. "Should we tell Mrs. Oldmeyer?" I asked.

"No." He took a couple gulps from a milk carton while staring at the ceiling, then wiped his mouth with his sleeve. "My people have suffered worse."

"What people," I said. "What are you talking about?"

"Persecution, Watson."

About a month later, at recess, Benjamin and I stood behind a circle of kids as Adam regaled them with the old Tony-smashed-Amy's-mailbox story. "I could drive a clutch better than that," he said. At one point he popped poor Gimp on the head, demonstrating how Mr. Cipriano had whacked Tony a couple of times with the rings on his sausage fingers. "He was G-R-O-U-N-D grounded," Adam said, rising up on his toes as he grinned.

Benjamin whispered to me, "Observe, Watson." Then shouting over my head, he said, "Does Tony know you squealed on him?"

Adam looked scared and plowed through the kids to face us. "Who says?"

"No one says."

"Was it Midge?" Adam shoved me, and I stumbled back, tripping and landing on my back as the bell rang.

"No way I squealed on Tony," he said walking away. "He'd murder me."

Benjamin extended his hand. He grinned, much like Adam had. "Sorry, Watson," he said as he helped me off the ground. "Retribution. It flows downhill." I looked up "retribution" that night.

A few days before Easter break, Benjamin's Science Fair entry — "The Effect of Ultraviolet Light on Microorganisms" — won the blue ribbon. He'd worked on it for weeks; a three-panel masterpiece. There were drawings of exploding nuclei and photographs of cottage-cheese-like organisms growing on blood agar in Petri dishes his father brought home from the lab. (Microbiologist was his father's "cover-job.") One dish looked like the super-secret bacteria destined for Khrushchev's orange juice.

I won an honorable mention for a project Benjamin had used in fourth grade — a model atom bomb. It wasn't much more than a star-pattern of dominoes, which exploded outward by tipping the center one over. "It's a metaphor," he said. Kids crowded the display in the cafeteria after lunch, setting up and knocking down the dominoes. To my delight, several of the popular girls thought the entertainment thrilling. After school on Thursday, Benjamin and I stopped by the cafeteria to set up the dominoes for Parents' Night, but the dominoes were gone.

"You know who took them," he said. We rushed to his display.

Someone had stuck small toy rats in the middle of the Petri dishes. On one, Benjamin's school picture was taped to the head. In red Magic-Marker a caption read *Mmmm good.*

Benjamin's shoulders slanted at a steeper angle than usual. I knew going to Mrs. Oldmeyer was out. "What are we going to do?" I said.

He collected the rats and threw them in the trash. The blood agar had depressions. He put the lids in place and arranged the dishes just so. On the bus ride home, he stared out the window for some time. Finally, he said, "Retribution, Watson. Retribution."

Friday evening, as we examined the schematic of the Andersons' and Ciprianos' backyards, he outlined the plan. "Our objective is to take a picture of Tony and Amy making out. That's Phase One."

"What about Adam?"

"That's Phase Two. It's best you stay in the dark in case you're captured during Phase One." He reached behind the encyclopedias and pulled out a Kodak Instamatic.

"That's Adam's camera," I said.

"Nope. It's mine," he said.

"You stole it?"

"I bought it — for the Science Fair." He extended his long neck. "Makes sense, doesn't it?"

～

Each morning during Easter Break we'd meet at the safe house, an army surplus tent pitched under the huge ash tree in Benjamin's backyard. He'd equipped the tent with a couple of sleeping bags, a battery-powered lantern, a Kellogg's Variety Pak, and a canteen of water. On one of those mornings, we perched in the tree until Mrs. Grant stopped puttering around her garden and took Patsy for a walk. Then we entered through the dog door and appropriated two fudgesicles. But on the way back, Benjamin grabbed her gardening gloves from the patio table. "Try these on."

The tips extended a half-inch past my fingers. "What for?"

"My mom tossed one of her pairs yesterday."

"So?"

"Patience, Watson. They're for Phase Two."

The whole week was about patience. We did nothing but camp out in the safe house, Headquarters, or the alley while we waited for Tony to jump the fence to Amy's.

On Friday, back at Headquarters after a fudgesicle and Rice Krispies breakfast, I selected a *Life* magazine from Benjamin's collection (the one with Oswald on the cover) and flopped onto his neatly made bed. Benjamin sat at his desk, his father's binoculars slung over the chair's back, and soldered transistors and diodes into a Heathkit radio. He hoped to communicate with Tel Aviv someday.

"Benjamin, what does this mean?" I pulled my midterm progress report from my pocket. Mrs. Oldmeyer had written "lacks initiative" in the comment section.

He rested the soldering iron in its cradle and took the paper. "It means you lack enthusiasm and leadership, Watson. It means planning isn't your forte." I think he sensed a lack of resolve on my part, perhaps some trepidation, because he added, "But it also implies you're quiet. Nearly invisible. A perfect spy."

That last part helped.

If Tony was going to make a move on Amy it wouldn't be until his mom ran errands. Every so often I sat up and looked out the side window. The Andersons' reciprocating sprinkler was catching the edge of the Ciprianos' carport with each pass. Mr. C's truck was gone and wouldn't return until five-thirty, when the odor of boiling tar followed him into the neighborhood. But Mrs. C's VW Beetle was still there, its front bumper banded to the frame with wire. That poor Bug. It really groaned under the weight of the Ciprianos when they chugged off to church each Sunday.

After a couple of hours, Mrs. C drove away. Benjamin tucked the camera inside his shirt, grabbed the binoculars, and said, "Let's move."

In the alley, we leaned our backs against the Ciprianos' fence, ate grapefruit plucked from the Andersons' overhanging trees, and shot loogies. I had just drawn a line in the warm dirt, where his phlegm beat my earlier effort, when he whispered, "Shh."

It was the sound of the trampoline.

I knee-walked over to an opening in the fence. "It's only Adam," I said.

Adam tried a back flip and landed on his knees. He made a few more attempts and then stopped to use his inhaler. We remained low and close to the fence. Benjamin cleaned the binoculars' lenses with his T-shirt.

The Ciprianos' yard didn't have grass. It was nothing but holes and mounds of dry earth, dug by Adam and maybe Tony when he was younger. The yard looked like the pictures in Benjamin's Time-Life books: Normandy Beach after D-Day. The swing set no longer had swings, only a couple of chains hanging from a rusting crosspiece. An old charcoal grill had fallen head first into one of the holes. Some of the holes had been backfilled over the years. They were now graves for former Cipriano pets — a cat next to a rabbit next to a parakeet — valiant fighters who no doubt succumbed to the care of the Cipriano boys. The lone pet survivor was Brutus, their Bassett hound. He contributed to the landscape with a minefield of logs. One time, Benjamin and I had spied Adam taking swings at Brutus with the shovel he used to clean up the dog's mess. When he tired of that, he spear-chucked the shovel into a hole, lay on his back in the dirt, and clapped his hands for Brutus. The dog had bounded over and plastered Adam's ears with sloppy kisses while Adam turned his head from side to side and giggled, actually giggled. No kid at school would have believed it.

A door slammed. "Hey, Wheezy, get off the tramp." It was Tony. "Make me, Butt-wipe."

Tony took a running leap and landed on the padded edge of the trampoline. We'd heard he was a diving star, although the only diving we'd seen him do were cannon-balls into the chilly water of the Anderson's above-ground pool. He wore sneakers, jeans, and a T-shirt that said AAA JR. NATIONAL DIVING CHAMPIONSHIPS across the front. "Get off. I need it."

"No, watch this."

Tony tackled Adam to the mat. He straddled him, grabbed the inhaler from Adam's pocket and held it out. "You want this back?"

"I'm going to tell Mom."

"Yeah, and I'll tell her you've been bouncing on the tramp again."

Tony threw the inhaler. It landed in the hole next to the dead charcoal grill. Adam squirmed free and jumped off the tramp. Tony stood on one edge, took a running step-and-a-half, and sprang up and off the far end of the mat.

"There he goes," I whispered. Tony's feet sailed over the fence and his body disappeared into the Andersons' backyard, followed by a thud as he landed on the grass. Even though I'd seen him leap before, it always amazed me. Such daring, even for a ninth grader.

Adam climbed back onto the trampoline. He yelled at

Tony at the peak of each leap. "I'm going to tell Dad...you went to Amy's."

Tony shouted back. "You do and I'll cram that pacifier up your ass."

Adam crawled off the tramp and righted his Sting-Ray from a pile of dirt. The baseball trading cards rat-a-tat-tatted as he rode out through their side gate.

We scurried to a position behind the Andersons' fence and manned the view-holes. Tony and Amy held hands in the sliding-glass doorway. She wore an oversized gray T-shirt with WEST HIGH across the front. When she placed her arms around Tony's neck, the shirt's bottom edge rose to the pockets of her cut-offs. She led Tony inside.

"Should we go?" I said.

"Patience, Watson." He drew deep from the back of his throat, turned, and shot a monster. It left a crater. "We'll wait until they're on the couch."

The air was mostly still. An occasional breeze lifted Adam's fake motorbike sound over the roofs to our position in the alley. Finally, Benjamin gave the word. We used the metal trash cans to boost ourselves up onto Amy's fence. We laid low under the overhanging grapefruit trees and scooted along the fence's two-by-four cap. We hopped down into her yard and hid behind the above-ground swimming pool. As expected, Amy hadn't closed the curtains across the double-wide doors.

Benjamin rested the binoculars on the metal edge of the pool and worked the focus.

"What do you see?" I said.

"Total concentration."

He handed me the binoculars, dropped completely behind the pool, and retrieved the camera from inside his shirt.

I adjusted the focus. Tony and Amy were making out. There was a semi-thrashing quality to their kissing...then something new. "He put his hand up her shirt!"

"Time to move in, Watson."

The television show *Combat!* had trained me for the next thing — how a soldier or spy crawls along the ground with a Gila Monster motion. I slithered across the yard and over a garden hose, my head down, the damp grass cooling my elbows and soaking the knees of my jeans. I was at the two-inch rise to the concrete patio when Benjamin clicked twice with his tongue. I froze and turned my head. Benjamin had ducked behind the pool. Tony and Amy must have disengaged. I closed my eyes tight, willing Tony to stay on the couch. No way could I outrun him. Then Benjamin gave me the one-click *all clear*. I moved forward and hunched behind a love-seat swing and potted palm tree. I was close enough to hear Beatles' music bleeding through the glass. And when I peered around the trunk, I was close enough to see Amy, naked from her waist up.

The sun, now cutting under the patio overhang, illuminated her left breast to a brilliant white, searing onto my eleven-year-old retinas an indelible image — Tony's hand swirling over Amy's breast like a fortune teller caressing the future. I forgot about the camera and just gazed. I felt no shame or embarrassment, only something resembling privilege. But after a few moments, a kind of anger crept under my skin. It was as if Adam had stolen my Willie Mays card and attached it to his spokes. I have experienced jealousy since, but this was a younger, more ephemeral version, and it was interrupted by a sound — a screeching crow. It was Benjamin, calling to me, and I remembered I was a spy, and this was a serious operation. He pumped his clenched fist in the air — the take-the-picture sign.

I rose to my knees long enough to aim the Instamatic between a palm frond and chain of the swing. I was disappointed to see how small Amy's breast looked in the viewfinder. I clicked the photo, slumped back behind the pot, and advanced the film. Benjamin gave the sign again. Up again. Click. I shot the entire roll, all twelve frames. He gave me the thumbs-up, waving me in.

We hustled over the fence and ran down the alley to the safe house. Out of breath, Benjamin complimented my stealth. We passed the canteen back and forth and laughed as we relived the day. I was indeed a perfect spy. After a time, we heard Mrs. Cipriano's voice. It arched through the light breeze and perfumed air of late afternoon. "Aaaa-duuum...Aaaa-duuum," she chanted — sung like a call to prayer for her youngest child. I'll never forget that.

The next day, Saturday night after dinner, we sat cross-legged on sleeping bags in the safe house and swigged Cokes while examining the *Top Top Secret* notebook under the light of the lantern. Our shadows projected as towering figures against the canvas wall. Benjamin had drawn and labeled the rooms of the Cipriano house. He popped the film cartridge from the Instamatic. "Tomorrow, we put this inside Adam's camera."

I didn't know how that was possible.

"In the morning, the Ciprianos go to church," he said. "We go into Adam's room and find his camera. We switch cartridges. We leave."

"I'm not supposed to go inside their house," I said.

"Watson, we're spies. In and out, like at Mrs. Grant's. No one knows."

"Why do we have to switch cartridges?"

Benjamin drew four rectangles in a row and labeled them *Woolworth's*, *Mr. C*, *Tony*, and *Adam*. Then he pointed to each as he explained. "Adam takes the film to Woolworth's. They develop it and call Mr. Cipriano. Mr. Cipriano annihilates Tony. Tony annihilates Adam."

"Dominoes," I said.

"Yes!" His face glowed in the lamplight. My skin

buzzed because I'd recognized the metaphor. And now this was as much my operation as his. *Retribution.* The word was as sweet as the night air. Adam will go to school with a black eye and fat lip and start lamenting to his chums, panning for sympathy. He'll say, "I didn't take those pictures. I don't know who did."

"'Puddin' Tain' I'll call out. Maybe even put my lunch tray down and pantomime a camera to my eye. 'Puddin' Tain.'"

Sunday morning, shadows from the ash tree's limbs swayed across the backlit canvas ceiling. We skipped a trip to Mrs. Grants' and ate quickly from the Variety Pak. The breezes from earlier in the week had strengthened to gusty winds, rippling the safe house walls. Outside, it was a blue-sky day. When the VW chugged away, we exited through Benjamin's gate, raced along the alley, and hopped the Ciprianos' fence. We wove our way through the bombed-out backyard and the Brutus logs. A dust devil swirled dried blossoms and dead leaves before collapsing against Adam's once sparkling Sting-Ray. The shovel that Adam used to threaten Brutus lay in front of the kitchen door. Benjamin handed me Mrs. Grant's gardening gloves and donned a pair of his own. We looked like Mickey and Minnie Mouse. He held his hands up. "No fingerprints, Watson." Then he moved the shovel aside and wiggled the doorknob. It was locked.

Benjamin crawled through the dog door, and as I followed him through, Brutus licked my face. The kitchen smelled like bacon. We found a blackened strip on a greasy paper towel and gave it to Brutus. He trotted to his pillow in the corner near the breakfast table. They had left the TV on in the family room (a guy with a beard was giving a painting lesson) and the couch cushions were lined up on the floor. We crept down the hall toward Adam's bedroom. The lights were on in the hall and also in Tony's room, where he'd hung a poster of Raquel Welch. Diving trophies lined the full length of a shelf.

If Benjamin was nervous, he didn't show it. That helped calm me, as did the sight of Adam's room. I guess I was expecting something dark and evil, not a room that looked like mine. The bedspread hung off-kilter. There were plastic models of war planes and an aircraft carrier on a shelf. A baseball bat with glove leaned against the wall. I bet he could hit.

Benjamin told me to check the closet.

The shelf was too high, but I looked under a pile of clothes. "It's not in here," I said.

Benjamin was searching the dresser. He waved Adam's underwear like a flag before closing the drawer. Then he lifted a green T-shirt off the desk and said, "Look at this." He aimed Adam's inhaler at me, gave a squirt, and set it down. He looked around the room. "Where would you hide a camera, Watson?" He felt behind a stack of *Mad* magazines on the shelf and found a transistor radio, which he examined front and back.

That's when a toilet flushed. Then a cough. We ran

into the hall and came face to wide-eyed face with Adam. Everyone froze. Adam wore only white briefs and socks. He didn't look nearly as formidable in his underwear. He was holding his fisted hand to his mouth, his eyebrows nearly connecting in the middle. His face and upper chest were the color of a plum until he took a deep breath and his more natural always-tan look returned.

Without a word Benjamin and I took off down the hall and through the family room. I was right behind Benjamin when he opened the kitchen door. Adam was coughing and yelling, "Rat, you goddamn rat, I'll kill you." I heard him slip on the kitchen linoleum, hit the floor, and cuss some more. I was half-a-dozen steps outside before I looked back and realized Adam wasn't behind me. I stopped. The kitchen door had closed automatically. The wind came in fierce gusts, whipping up more and more dirt from the Ciprianos' yard. I squinted between the fingers of the gloves. Brutus romped out the dog door with a sock in his mouth. When Adam still didn't show, I glanced at the fence. Benjamin was scrambling over the top. I knelt to pet Brutus and was wondering if I should check on Adam when the kitchen door flew open. Adam's eyes bulged like a maniac's. "I'll get you!"

He grabbed the shovel and ran straight for me.

I vaulted onto the trampoline and took a half bounce, imagining Adam behind me about to take a Babe-Ruthian swing at my ankles. It was my first experience with adrenaline, and by the next full bounce, I was maximally charged. I blasted over the fence. My view from the sky was of Benjamin standing in the alley, a look of astonishment on his rat-face as his Mickey-Mouse-like protégé descended upon him. He broke my fall just enough so my legs didn't snap.

For a moment we listened for Adam, for clambering or cursing behind the sound of the wind. We didn't hear him, so we peeked through the fence. All we could see were his legs sticking out of the dog door. Brutus licked the foot without the sock.

"Hah," Benjamin said. "He got locked out."

Jubilant despite our failed mission, we ran back to the safe house and worked on an alibi for when Adam told his parents, who undoubtedly would tell ours. We had only one explanation — Adam was a liar.

Adam did not tell his parents.

I did not witness his last breaths in the kitchen where his mother found him. I did not hear the wheezing, the gasps for air — sounds I imagined later as I grew older — but I heard the wail that accompanied his passing. It came while Benjamin and I were sitting on sleeping bags in the safe house, cloaked in secrecy behind the canvas walls. The wail ascended with the dust and scattered grapefruit blossoms from the Ciprianos' yard. It began at a low pitch, scooped a little lower, then eased higher and higher like a plea from Benjamin's mournful cello. I can hear it still. It repeats and repeats and repeats. It is Brutus.

Benjamin tapped the film cartridge on his knee and shook his head. "He better cut that out, or Adam will cream him with the shovel." Then he raised his rat-face to the leafy shadows dancing on the canvas ceiling, extended his long neck, and howled. He howled and howled, and it seemed to only irritate Brutus, who howled even louder, and the whole concert of howling spooked me. I didn't know Adam was dead, but I knew something was wrong, like I knew Adam was trouble when I spied the baseball cards on his spokes. I knew in the mysterious way a body knows a thing before words try to deny it.

I wanted to go home.

When I walked out of the tent, Benjamin followed. "Where you going?" he said.

I didn't answer. If I did, I thought I might cry. I opened the gate.

"We're spies, Watson. We keep secrets. No matter what Adam says, we weren't there." He waved the cartridge in my face.

I grabbed it — I don't know why — and ran.

Within an hour, Mrs. C was at our front door, pounding frantically and screaming my father's name, but he was at the hospital.

For the remainder of that horrible day, my mother cried — on the phone, standing at the kitchen sink peeling carrots, looking out the front window to the police cars and ambulance across the street. I didn't ask her what was going on. And I suspect she was relieved she didn't have to tell me. Mostly, I cleaned my room as was my responsibility every Sunday. When my father returned that night, he spent some time at the Ciprianos'. We had soup for dinner. Between ladled bites, my mother touched my face, or arm, and did the same to my little sister and baby brother. After dinner, my parents put my siblings in front of the TV and motioned for me to follow them to the living room. I sat between them on the couch. "You understand what happened today, Rick?" my father began.

I shook my head, no.

In his slow, reassuring way, he told me what he learned from his visit to the Ciprianos' house, explaining that Adam's asthma was worse than his parents thought. The whole time he talked, I looked out the front window to Mr. C's truck, the VW, and two other cars that were parked in front. Lights lit the windows.

When he finally said, "Adam died, Rick." I swallowed hard. It was the only outward sign of the tight throat and jackhammer heart I hid behind my granite spy expression. For several moments, we sat in silence except for occasional audience laughter drifting in from the TV.

Then my mother leaned into me and drew my head to

her shoulder. "Ricky," she said. "You're healthy. You're going to be all right. Understand?"

I didn't understand, but I nodded anyway. I imagined my parents' admiration when I told them the truth. They'd understand that Adam wasn't supposed to die. We just wanted to get back at him for Puddin' Tain and pushing me down, stealing my dominoes, and all the rat stuff with Benjamin. I was lucky to get out alive, really. They'd be relieved for that and amazed at my athletic prowess when I described jumping the fence.

"Your mom says you spent the night in the tent at Benjamin's," my dad said. "Did you two hear anything coming from the Ciprianos' this morning?"

I thought about Benjamin mimicking Brutus and how it spooked me.

My mother angled away and held my shoulders at arm's length. "Anything at all. Amy thought she heard Adam yelling at someone, but she was half asleep."

There was such a look of hope in my mother's eyes.

My answer came naturally. I shook my head no.

"Are you sure?" Dad said.

"He yells at Brutus a lot."

Mom hugged my head to her breast and rocked and cried, and what she was thinking passed to me as clearly as if she'd spoken aloud — *You never disobey. You are such a good boy. Such a perfect son.*

～

It was months before the neighborhood settled into a new state of normal. Mrs. Oldmeyer took a leave of absence and never came back. Adam's toady friends huddled by the rings at recess and kicked the dirt, polishing rumors about Adam's death that shone like fact by seventh grade. The week after the funeral, Mr. C loaded his truck with the disassembled trampoline — the rails, the springs, the mat, and padding — and drove it all off somewhere. That April, he backed in a load of dirt and filled the holes. I don't know what happened to the Sting-Ray. Maybe he buried it. It was about that time that Tony and Amy broke up; at least, I never saw him in her back-yard. By May, the Ciprianos had moved out. My mom heard later, they divorced.

Neither Benjamin nor I attended Adam's funeral. That day, instead of playing tetherball after lunch, I sat with Benjamin in the shadow of the music room. It was a hot, blue afternoon. An account of the accident had appeared in the morning paper. Benjamin flattened the article against the sidewalk between his outstretched legs.

The paper said Adam had stayed home from church because of a cold. Most likely he went outside and bounced on the trampoline. Between the exercise, the dust, and his cold, his lungs shut down — *status asth-maticus*. It'd been known to happen. A tragic, tragic set of circumstances, the paper concluded.

My mother kept a copy of the paper in her purse for weeks.

"*Status Asthmaticus*," Benjamin said. "It sounds like the guy in *To Kill a Mockingbird*."

I didn't say anything.

"I'll give you the book. You should read it. It's all about persecution."

"Maybe."

"It means when people hate you because of who you are." He folded the article. "Like Adam hating Jews."

"He hated everybody," I said. "Except maybe Brutus, sometimes."

"Yes, but he hated Jews," he said. "I'm sure."

I smashed an ant that was threatening to crawl onto my sneakers. "I thought he was going to murder me with that shovel."

"You looked like Tony flying over the fence."

"Really?" I looked up.

He smiled, and it felt like we were back at Headquarters.

"What'd you do with the cartridge?"

"Smashed it with my dad's hammer."

He nodded in approval.

"What about the notebook?" I asked.

"Destroyed according to protocol."

When he extended his neck, I suspected he was lying, but either way, we were spies, and spies knew how to keep secrets. "I think we should go dark for a while," he said.

That was fine with me. Every time I looked at his rat-face, it reminded me of Adam. We never spied together again.

Late that night, unable to sleep, I rose from bed and parted my blinds. Across the street, a light was on in Amy's room. A few minutes later, a shadow passed by her curtain.

I retrieved the film cartridge from the shelf behind my desk. I'd done the same thing the night after Adam died, the night I convinced my mother I was still her perfect son. In bed, I rotated the cartridge between my fingers toward the stippled ceiling. *Amy's in there.*

I thought awhile about how I might someday develop the photographs. It would require patience and initiative. I closed my eyes and joined her. She smiles and purrs my name — Ricky. She places her arms around my neck. She likes that I am short and can soar over her fence like Tony. She loves my smile. *Did you know I can ride a unicycle and throw a curve ball?* I say. *A real bender.* She takes my hand and guides me to the couch. We lie down. She kisses me, always my first kiss, long and passionate. Then she removes her WEST HIGH shirt, hugs my head to her breast, and tells me I'll be all right. *You'll be all right, Ricky,* she says. *Understand?*

PART II

THE MIDDLE YEARS

HARVEST
PROSE POEM

The surgeon presses the scalpel deep to the breastbone and orders *Harvest the heart*. You might envision a man in a white lab coat plucking it from a tree, the ripest of all the hearts sagging the limbs in the heart orchard behind the hospital; next to the fields where kidneys grow in perfectly straight alternating rows of Left and Right, converging to a point past the horizon; near the experimental greenhouse where brains — and even consciousness itself — sprout tiny buds in climate-controlled bell jars.

But there are no farms and there is no growing season for human hearts. They arrive by chance. Mostly at a time when you are asleep and mothers pause before answering the phone. They tumble down gravel roads, buffered inside bony cages, and roll through automatic glass doors into emergency rooms, where they will be passed like gold batons, one at a time, from grief to hope to a waiting chest.

PLAYING DOCTOR

I t is 1977. Your eyes are closed. Your scrub pants have accordioned to your ankles, and the waistband of your plaid boxers stretches from knee to knee. *You are a professional.* You remind yourself of this, elbows indenting cool vinyl, while Celeste, your exam partner, the most stunning stripper, lab tech, vegetarian, medical student goddess to ever shake your clammy hand, now probes your prostate with her slender, latex-gloved index finger.

You are a "student of medicine, a professional." The Dean's words, in all their loftiness, still waggle at your conscience like an admonishing digit. You are more than a straight-A, doodle-in-the-margins guy; more than a baseball-card-collecting, artist-science-genius Hobbit who has been on exactly three dates since high school. Buried in your college past are jazz festival T-shirts and a shaggy haircut. Button-down collars, ties, and pants with cuffs sprout in your tiny apartment closet now. You wear a thirty-six-regular white doctor-coat. Every morning you add a little mousse to your hair and comb it back, like you did tonight. Celeste once said you shouldn't hide your green eyes.

Last year's class dubbed this "R & B Night." Rectals and breasts. Gentlemen first.

You smile. You think about the other nine gentlemen behind the other nine privacy curtains. Any one of them would pass a stone to trade postures with you. Outside your curtain, a female proctor asks, "Everything okay?"

Celeste and you respond in tandem, like a master ventriloquist and the dummy you are in her presence. "We're fine. We're fine."

For a student of medicine, Celeste is gentle. Because she is a student of medicine, she is thorough. "Left lobe — smooth without nodules." She says this softly, but with the same sultry throatiness that for the last eighteen months has sent a piloerector wave down your arm in multidisciplinary lab. You remember — that time you pointed to the red pushpins in the middle of the brain specimen and one by one she laid down a melody line: *amygdala, hippocampus,* the *cingulate gyrus?* Man, you riffed on the backs of those syllables all day long.

You anticipate pressure on the right lobe next. There it is. "Smooth without nodules," she says again. The hairs stand up on your anterior thigh. You think of her thighs — long, lean, tan — those ethereal thighs that vanish in your night-dreams before you can wrap them around your waist. You go farther in your daydreams, but not now. You think of baseball, spring training, and beer hawkers. You think of androgen-juiced patrons in muscle shirts and Ray-Bans, elbowing their buddies in the ribs as you sidestep past with Celeste, their eyes bubbling the sunscreen you'd applied to her bare, brown back. You should ask her out.

How many times are you going to imagine this? She would never go out with you. You are twenty-two. She is twenty-nine. You listen to Coltrane; she prefers The Eagles. If you ever slow-danced to "Desperado," she could rest her chin on your head. Her last boyfriend was a Triple-A shortstop who got the call to the majors; your glove is missing a lace between the fourth and fifth fingers. She nibbles on carrot-sticks out of a ziplock bag. You wolf Twinkies out of the box.

She draws blood at County on weekends. She wants to be a pediatrician and open a child crisis center someday; you're thinking sculpting bodies might be cool. She's seen your dissections and your drawings of the human hand. She said you could be a professional artist and showed you the yin-yang tattoo inked along the downy small of her back. She doesn't know you've drawn her during biochemistry. While she took notes from the front row and the professor eyed her ample cleavage, you sketched her profile: the square angle of her mandible, the high zygomatic arch she dusts with rouge, the

vermilion border of her lower lip, downturned and invit-
ing. You have other drawings of her, a regular portfolio.
What you can't see, you imagine.

Now she sweeps her finger a hundred eighty degrees.
You feel the pressure dorsally. Is the term dorsal or
ventral? Yes, it's dorsal, like dorsal fin. She has her other
hand on your back. Your bare heels lift half an inch from
the industrial-carpeted floor.

Celeste inquires about your comfort. You tell her you
are fine. You are fine to offer your rectum for her exami-
nation and medical edification. You were fine to share lab
space and a dual microscope during Pathology as you
both searched for cellular deviants. You were fine whenever she adjusted the focus (her fingers moved with the
grace of a geisha), particularly in the morning when, forehead to forehead, you inhaled the moist aroma of her
peach-scented conditioner.

One day, early on, while you both peered into the
microscope, she said you reminded her of her brother.
He's quiet, listens well, and reads all things Buddhist.
That's you — her best guy-friend.

For a year-and-a-half, you've used the microscope like
a telephone. You told her about your life. It didn't take
long. Yours is flat. Your dad's a doctor, your teeth are
perfect, and you ride to school on the same ten-speed you
had in college.

Her life is interesting: abortion at seventeen, parents
divorced then followed up by divorcing their kids. She

told you how she went from nothing (less than nothing by your standards) to college and then medical school, but only on the second try. She told you that stripping was her aunt's idea — money and contacts. Frat boys and jocks in a pulsing sweat handed over their allowance of twenties. Accountants, lawyers, and doctors lined her G-string with fifties, more for a private dance. They couldn't empty their wallets fast enough.

You love peering into the blue-hot core of her life. How could you not?

One time, she told you about an ambulance-chasing lawyer on TV who, several years ago, gave her five one-hundred-dollar bills. You asked her who. She wouldn't say. You admired her discretion. She adjusted the slide in the scope and without looking up, whispered, "Don't tell anyone, but we smoked a little dope in his hotel, and I gave him a promise...well a little more than a promise, and he gave me another five bills in the morning...we kept it very professional." When she asked if the slide looked focused to you, you didn't hear her at first. Your autonomic nervous system was a runaway blaze.

"I'm sorry, does that hurt?" she asks.

You realize your sphincter grips the proximal phalanx of her index finger like a boa on a mouse. You relax. "No," you say, and she exits. She snaps off her glove, and then hands you a tissue, before stepping away to wash her hands. You wipe your ass and pull up your pants.

You prepared for this night with a cool-wave body

wash and too much Paco Rabanne under your arms. God forbid you should sweat.

She returns, sits on the portable table, and lowers her head to untie the skinny bow behind her neck. She shivers. Her peasant blouse falls like a silk curtain at a museum — a masterpiece unveiled. Her breasts are unlike any breasts you've seen in three dimensions; unlike your high-school girlfriend whose modest breasts you only saw through Braille-like excursions under her blouse, or the impish breasts of the college drawing-class model. That is the sum of your experience. You are pathetic.

She straightens her back and folds her hands in her lap. Your turn, now.

Act like a professional. You memorized the routine. Begin with inspection. *Size and symmetry.* They are grand in proportion to her lithe frame. No fruit comparisons. That is more than crude; that's an injustice. Her left breast suspends so slightly, so gracefully lower than her right. *Contour.* You think of long strands of ribbons arcing through the air behind Chinese dancers — smooth, flowing. *The appearance of the skin.* Honey-toned within the privacy of her bikini line, an olive-brown beyond. *Inspect the nipples.* Cylindrical, demure. You love the way they tip slightly up to you, the areolae dark and contracted.

You have her raise her arms above her head, then after a moment have her press her hands against her hips. These are not breasts that dimple or retract. These are dream breasts. You will draw them when you draw her tonight, or tomorrow night, and the sun-streaked ringlets of hair that have fallen across her clavicles. You have a fine memory.

Palpation comes next, but she waits for your instruction.

"Would you please lie back," you say.

She asks you to hand her the towel. She lays it on the chilly vinyl. You castigate yourself for not thinking of her well-being. But you recover, and briskly rub your cold hands together, warming them, trying not to appear like a starving teen about to dive into a Thanksgiving feast.

She stares at the acoustic tiles on the ceiling. Her eyes are wide. As you touch the skin of her right breast, she tenses. "Was that cold?" you say.

She doesn't turn her head, just her eyes — a brief sweep across your gaze, accompanied by a thin smile — almost as if she's embarrassed. "No, you're doing fine," she says.

You work systematically, covering all four quadrants with the three-finger rotary motion you practiced on a thawed bag of peas last night. You compress the tissue against her chest wall. You are working with Braille again. You close your eyes, diving to the tips of your fingers, your right brain in a lazy backstroke across her ribbony contours and honeyed skin. There is depth now, pristine firmness and elasticity that transcend the constituent fat and fiber. It undulates beneath your touch; it massages something primitive in your midbrain as your exam spirals toward her areola. It is at this point that you are allowed to lightly pinch her nipple between your thumb and index finger. You do this, focused on the tiny ducts, not expecting a sign of trouble. There is none, except for the urge to flick her taut nipple with your tongue.

Careful. Turn your attention (it's what doctors say) to her left breast. You proceed methodically, cautiously this time. And as you approach the end of your exam, you fall against the disconsolate truth that you will never again see these breasts or touch this body beyond tonight. But with that, a drunken thought staggers to light: for some, what was the prelude to a five-hundred-dollar privilege, for you, had been included in the cost of tuition. You are the envy of your testosterone-charged classmates. You finish the exam, mentally high-fiving yourself, yet in your best doctor-voice, you say, "Everything feels fine."

You start to raise her blouse, but she stops you. In the privacy of your make-believe doctor's office, she tenderly grasps your hand. You feel her thumb against the soft flesh behind the pads of your fingers. She presses them to her right breast. "Do you feel that?" she says.

"What?" you say.

"Do you feel a lump?" She guides your fingers with hers.

You think you feel it. You place her hands at her sides. You examine deep, beneath her areola. There is something. Small. Maybe round and somewhat firm. It doesn't feel mobile, but you can't quite tell. You pull back. You palpate again. Yes, there's definitely something there, something you missed the first time, and it's raising a knot inside your chest.

Her chocolate irises dilate. She says her doctor wants to biopsy it; that's the next step. But you're not thinking about next steps or options. These are things that become ingrained in you a few years later, during your general surgery training, and later still, as a plastic surgeon. Right now you're thinking of Pathology lab and all the cancers you and Celeste examined under the microscope: ugly, anonymous tissue that she dialed into focus with her graceful fingers.

You missed it. But medical students miss lumps. That's not why you call yourself a worthless piece of shit as you pedal home in the darkness. It's not why you tear up your drawings of her, the things you call art, and then throw them in the dumpster out back along with the dozen, carbon-graphite pencils you bust in half.

Not exactly. You do it because of what she said after you helped her sit up, after you retied the skinny bow behind her neck.

Celeste straightened her back, extended her hand, and said something in a voice as trusting and sweet as a tenor sax, something that blended with her peachy scent to haunt the depth of your brain long after her passing. "Thank you. That was very professional."

WHAT THE DOCTOR DIDN'T KNOW

The first time William T. Barnes, M.D. had been a patient, he was not yet a doctor. Back during the summer between college and medical school, on a day near the end of what he would describe as the sweet spot of his life, he underwent surgery to position his lower jaw back a quarter inch. Bill saw it this way: he had a small problem; it could become a bigger problem; it needed to be fixed. At the conclusion of surgery, stainless steel wires banded his upper and lower teeth together at six points along the arc of his new smile. He lay asleep on the gurney, his head elevated, his breathing steady, the only patient in the recovery room on a tranquil afternoon, and in the post-operative fog there were things he didn't know.

He didn't know that his lips were dry. He didn't perceive the damp chill of the ice bags on the sides of his swollen face. He didn't register the click of his wife's shoes on the linoleum when she walked in, didn't smell the dental office on her hygienist uniform, or hear the recovery room nurse whisper, "Things went well," as the nurse disposed of an empty morphine syringe. He did not feel his wife stroke his hand, nor see his wedding band parked safely on her middle finger. When she kissed his forehead, her relief failed to penetrate the anesthetic mist that bathed him.

Bill was twenty-two. This was only a month after their wedding and two weeks after they moved into a single-level one-bedroom in student housing. She'd planted purple and pink petunias in the three-foot by three-foot square below the bedroom window. He'd cut two four-foot shelves from walnut-veneered plywood, mounted them to the wall using black metal brackets, and then loaded those shelves with the first fifty pounds or so of what he had yet to learn: anatomy, histology, and human development for the first semester; physiology, biochemistry, and neuroanatomy for the second. Below the shelves and on top of an old whiskey barrel, they placed a forlorn thirteen-inch Toshiba.

The night before his hospital admission, they turned the TV off after the Bicentennial fireworks. In bed, she shed her nightgown under the covers and rolled on top of Bill. Using her index finger, she traced his lower lip, kissed it, and traced it again. "Are you nervous?" she asked.

He lined up where he was with where he was headed, and envisioned the passage to be as lucent and unswerving as his draw to her. When he said he wasn't worried, she repeated a phrase she'd said many times before — *you're a brick* — and then made love to the old smile.

Now, in the recovery room, she traced his lips again, and then smoothed a few wayward hairs on his dark mustache. He didn't know she was comparing the old look to the new, trying to picture his face without the swelling.

He didn't know that in fourteen years — half a career after the swelling subsided — his face would readily shift to a look of incredulity. During the narcotic usage audit at Red Mountain Community Hospital, he would give the committee that look; then, he'd voluntarily step away as Anesthesiology Department Chairman when the findings were inconclusive. A little later, he would take a week off from work — it was the flu again. One afternoon that week, a hardened version of his wife stood at the bedside, opened her hand, and showed him a glass ampule of fentanyl. She'd discovered the narcotic in the workshop adjacent to their three-car garage.

"I was looking for a wrench," she said. "To tighten the

loose faucet because I can't seem to get you to do anything around here anymore."

"Babe," he said, "I don't know what you're talking about."

She shattered the ampule against the headboard. "Enough, Billy!" She retreated a few steps, lowered her head, and hugged her chest as if she were naked and cold. In a small, jagged voice, she said, "You used to be my brick."

He didn't know that when she'd say those words, the bones in his face would crumble, or that he'd enter rehab in Sierra Vista the next day.

Several months before her words would trigger the rebuilding, he understood that settling a malpractice case didn't necessarily settle your mind. The newspapers would publish his name. Surgeons would book fewer cases. Sleep would avoid him, but when it did arrive, the face of the boy and voice of the boy's father penetrated his dreams. Leftover Percocet from his wife's surgery lent relief. When that ran out, he tried IV fentanyl. His training would make it safe. He didn't know that squirreling away 2 ml — and then 5 ml — amps could be so simple. At the hospital, a syringe filled with normal saline would be labeled *fentanyl*; the ampules would go in his briefcase.

Asleep in the recovery room, he didn't know that the first of his two sons would be born in four years. The boys would hit all the milestones on the growth chart and play Little League. Most years, he signed out on a rich March afternoon, pulled them from school, and lathered their faces and arms with sunscreen for a Giants' spring training game. He'd drive thirty miles to Scottsdale Stadium in a Jeep with the top down. He bought the boys peanuts, red vines, and baseball caps that folded their ears. The same year his sons would turn nine and seven, the coroner's report would conclude that a two-year-old patient of his had had undiagnosed Duchenne's muscular dystrophy.

But now, before he'd begun his medical training, Bill didn't know that ninety-eight percent of the body's potassium lay sequestered safely inside the cells. He didn't know that succinylcholine, a neuromuscular blocker he would later use every day at work, could cause diseased muscle cells to crack open. The flood of potassium could silence a beating heart the way water snuffs a fire. He didn't know that that year, his two-year-old patient would be one of five in the United States to succumb to the same scenario.

Bill didn't know that a week before the coroner's report, he would be dressed in green scrubs, moist with sweat. He'd check the clock, and in an ailing and fragile hand, record the time of death as 14:52. After the OR cleared, while he waited alone for the surgeon to return with the boy's father, he stopped thinking like a doctor. He pulled the endotracheal tube from the child's mouth — no father should have to see that.

The dad, wearing the same T-shirt and painters' pants from an hour before, ran screaming into the operating room. The feral rocking and twisting of the young man over the tiny, dusky face of the boy sucked muscle and bone from Bill. He would quiver as he watched the man clutch the child. Strings of saliva and mucous dripped from the father's lips and nose. "You killed my boy! You killed my boy!"

Bill didn't know that in some small measure, he would agree.

His jaw surgery came before he would know the algorithms of advanced cardiac life support. It came before he performed a standard IV induction and intubation on a two-year-old boy. After confirming breath sounds in each lung, he taped the endotracheal tube in place, adjusted the vaporizer, and was about to tell the surgeon the funny comment the father had made in the holding area. Then, two different alarms went off. The boy's color turned to steel. A flat line drifted across the EKG, and that shouldn't have been — couldn't have been

— happening. There had to be some other explanation. Then a third alarm sounded. He called a code, turned off the vaporizer, and directed the surgeon to start chest compression.

He didn't know this would happen on a Saturday, the sole case in the four-room OR suite. Two recovery nurses hurried with the crash cart. There wasn't another anesthesiologist in the house, and the ER physician was busy with his own cases.

He didn't know how foreign the milligram-per-kilogram calculations of epinephrine, bicarb, calcium, and atropine could seem when the whole situation was foreign — a cardiac arrest in a healthy child — something he would only occasionally rehearse for in his head. He didn't know that, during a crisis, even the students who were bricks would battle panic as well as the problem itself. What next? What have I forgotten? More epi. Draw labs. Another IV? Get more help. Why now? Why me? This isn't working. What did I miss? What did I miss? What will I say?

Bill didn't know that at 1:30 on a Saturday afternoon call day, he would meet a young father in the pre-op holding area. Drooling and clutching at his dad's white T-shirt, the man's two-year-old son sat crosslegged on a stretcher. Bill's notes on the patient's history would say that the boy had eaten Cheerios at 8 a.m. He and the boy's father chatted and, at one point, the conversation turned to baseball. The man was a Giants' fan, and Bill mentioned that he wasn't supposed to be on call, but had switched so that he could take in the Cubs and Giants on Sunday with his two sons.

The ENT surgeon strode into the room and interrupted. "Let me show you what we've got." He would hold an x-ray to the fluorescent lights and use his pen to tap at the two white ovals trapped in the child's upper esophagus. "There are the pennies. This should only take about five minutes." Bill, relieved that he might get home early, would nod.

When the OR was ready, the father would smooth the boy's blond hair, unclench the tiny fists, and entrust him to Bill, saying, "It's okay, Chad," as the child's confused pleas crescendoed in Bill's ear. Then the father would add, "Daddy'll be right here when you get back."

It was a reassurance Bill had heard parents make hundreds of times. Just like always, this boy's dad had bounced the child in his arms and begin telling him a story about Bert and Ernie and a big mess. And just before Bill had turned the corner into the OR, the father had said something funny from behind him, something Bill had never heard before. "Hey, Doc, keep the change."

~

Bill didn't know that before that Saturday, he'd care for about a thousand patients a year in private practice and guide each of them in for a safe landing. About every fourth night, he wouldn't make it home in time for dinner or to kiss his wife and sons goodnight. He didn't know that during his fellowship, a seventy-six-year-old woman with a leaking thoracic aneurysm would look up at him before he put the mask on her face and say, "Please don't let me die." But she would.

He didn't know that as a senior resident, he'd forget to try a simple device when he was unable to breathe for a gunshot victim during emergency surgery. The surgeon would save the patient's life with a tracheotomy. Despite that, nine months later, Bill would be voted outstanding resident in his class.

He didn't know that as a fourth-year medical student, he'd be third author on a paper describing the pharmacokinetics of fentanyl in obese patients. He didn't know that as a third-year student, he'd successfully intubate a patient for the first time after failing on four others. And he didn't know that when his second year began and his plywood shelves sagged with yet more books, tucked between Goodman and Gillman's 1,843-page *Pharmacological Basis of Therapeutics* and Robbins' 1,595-page *Pathological Basis of Diseases* would be a thin primer entitled *Preparation for Clinical Medicine*.

Bill's wife slid his ring back onto his finger. She smiled and moistened his lips with Vaseline. Underneath the skin, at the angle of his jaw, the severed ends of nerve fibers sizzled and sparked. Their electric warnings sped along a chain of ion channels and neurotransmitters. They leapt across synapses in the spinal cord and then careened upward through the brainstem. They streaked along ancient phylogenic pathways in the midbrain, past distant folds of gray matter, young and malleable and waiting for all the things he didn't know. Aiming for the cerebral cortex, the neural lightning cleared the last synaptic junction in the thalamus, and then accelerated before crashing into a thick wall of morphine and residual anesthesia.

Behind the wall and bathed in the mist, Bill was as far from the pain as he was close.

SECTION

I was still in scrubs, the weight of thirty-six hours in the hospital anchoring my bones to a chair in the OB nursing station, when a shriek like a Confederate charge — *Ay-yi-yi-yi-yi-yi-yi* — tore through the wall of room 626. It was past 7:00 p.m. Diaz was in the room, pleading with Lupe, his seventeen-year-old primiparous patient, to finally accept an epidural. The anesthesiologist taking over for me wouldn't be up for another thirty minutes. He was finishing a hip fracture downstairs. I was hoping to get home before Maggie put the boys to bed.

I slid to the seat's edge, unwrapped a Tootsie Roll Pop, and set my feet on the counter. The unit secretary pushed away from her computer terminal, turned, and glared at me over her reading glasses. "Good gracious, how much longer are we going to have to listen to that?"

Lupe's wail had penetrated wood, plaster, and steel all

afternoon, every three minutes. Yet her mother was adamant: "No needle in the back of *mi hija*." She'd had a friend whose sister's friend had an aunt who was para- lyzed after a spinal or some such nonsense. Frankly, I was hoping she'd offer her proxy refusal again. I was spent. As a favor, I'd covered the main operating rooms the night before. Between a lady with a drill bit poking through her hand and an old guy with a dead bowel who required an epinephrine drip to scrape his blood pressure off the floor, I never shut my eyes. Then, in the morning, I took over OB call.

I had hoped to catch a little sleep in a spare room. That didn't pan out. Just after I showered and put on a fresh set of scrubs, Bonnie, the nurse anesthetist on duty, called me with the first admission of the day, Eliz- abeth Renke, a multiparous patient who'd waddled in for an induction of labor. I stopped by her room before breakfast. Searching for the fetal heartbeat, the nurse was roaming a hockey-puck-like transducer over Eliza- beth's exposed abdomen. I began my "I'm the anesthe- siologist on call" spiel, but Elizabeth halted me with both arms extended like a traffic cop and announced with a smile, "I'm here for the Cadillac treatment. No more natural childbirth, especially since I finally get my girl."

She'd risen early for this. There was some serious care taken in the application of mascara and shadow, and her brunette hair, coiffed in loopy waves past her shoulder, had that CoverGirl sheen. She gazed up to her husband standing at her side.

He wore a white shirt with a pink tie and exuded the fresh-squeezed morning aroma of Old Spice. On the tie, the phrase IT'S A GIRL! screamed vertically in italic black from his buckle to his collar. She gripped his hand and they smiled at each other, and if this had been a cartoon, little hearts would have danced from their eyes. Then she looked back at me. "So, I'm ready for that epidural any time."

The nurse located the heartbeat, and the machine's tinny speaker emitted a sound like a wooden mallet striking a coconut a hundred-thirty-eight times a minute. Using broad elastic bands, she cinched the transducer in place. "Why don't we get you in labor first?"

"Of course," Elizabeth said. "I was just saying, whenever you...I mean whenever he...oh, I don't know what I'm saying. I'm just so excited to see little Kaylee."

"Kaylee Ann," her husband added.

They glanced at the display on the monitor, then back to each other and squeezed out a few more bouncy hearts. Elizabeth then shooed her husband off to work, reminding him that her mother would take two of their boys to school and watch the third at home.

I filled her order for a Cadillac epidural at about noon.

She panted through the contractions, concluding each one with a full deep breath — a cleansing breath, the labor coaches call it. By the time I finished charting, she had the phone to her ear, talking to her husband. The nurse pointed to a contraction wave on the monitor. Elizabeth looked at it, then down to her abdomen, then over to me, and chatting away, smiled with a wink and a thumbs-up. As my shift was ending, Elizabeth was still laboring, but Bonnie said she was close. For the day, though, I'd had eight patients deliver — six labor epidurals and two C-sections — all girls. I'd had busy days on OB before, but not a day when each patient I touched delivered a girl. Eight healthy baby girls.

I sucked on the Tootsie Pop and contemplated this statistical oddity. Since we'd found out Maggie was pregnant again, my mind had been filled with statistics. I couldn't remember ever participating in the live birth of a child who was not healthy. I don't mean a kid that came out blue because the cord prolapsed or the placenta separated, but one with a congenital anomaly — small round ears, a fish mouth, a webbed neck. The kinds of deformities that trigger a second glance at the mall. I'd seen none of that, not during my four years of residency or eight years of private practice. What were the odds? I didn't know, but I imagined myself on a giant swing, paused at the peak of its arc, waiting to descend.

"Doctor, did you ever call your wife back?" The unit secretary's bark startled me.

"Oh, shit." I dropped my feet to the floor and reached for the phone.

"You know, I just love listening to that British accent of hers," she said. "Gives me goosebumps. How far along did you say she is?"

"I didn't," I said, forming the words around the Tootsie Pop before pulling it out. "Now, please don't tell anyone else." That was futile. When a secret entered the hospital, it spread like drug-resistant bacteria.

Just then, Diaz emerged from room 626. He looked pregnant himself in the yellow gown that covered his slacks, shirt, and tie. He held a printout from the fetal heart monitor and pointed out something to Bonnie, sitting on a chair by the nurse's station. While nodding, she pulled a disposable bouffant cap from her purse and stretched it over her perm. I had a bad feeling.

Diaz looked up and said, "Section."

The unit secretary cheered. I tomahawked the Tootsie Pop toward the trash. As the candy left my hand, it slipped and sailed high, past her ear, shattering against the wall into a dozen violet candy crystals.

"Jesus, Doctor, no need to take it out on me," she said. "I just transcribe the orders, I don't give them."

Without speaking or looking at her, I began to pick the candy shards out of the tiered baskets of forms on her desk. She grabbed my wrist, turned me around, and gave me a shove toward Diaz. "Just go take care of that little screamer."

Diaz waved the tracing at me. "Sorry, bro. Just come look at these decels."

I didn't have to. I could trust my own wife's OB. As I moved past him toward Lupe's room, I tapped on the tracing. "It's going to be a girl, you know."

Lupe, a slight seventeen-year-old, whimpered while her boyfriend, Antonio — his name was inscribed on his shirt's breast pocket below SANDY'S AUTOMOTIVE — clasped her hands and whispered in her ear. The mother slouched splay-legged in a chair, a washcloth on her head.

Bending toward Lupe, I explained in a low voice what a spinal anesthetic involved. I paused while she vise-gripped Antonio's hand and thrashed through another contraction and practiced her rebel yell. When she relaxed, Antonio massaged his fingers. There were faint grease stains deep in the cuticles, impossible to get clean in a single scrubbing. I knew from restoring my MG.

"Cross them like this," I said. And I showed him how I had crossed my first and middle fingers for Maggie during her labors. "This way it doesn't hurt so much when she squeezes."

While the nurses readied Lupe and the C-section room, I walked down the hall to the doctor's lounge. I had at least ten minutes. The lounge was empty. A high school football game blared on the TV. I found the remote on the couch, hidden under the scattered remnants of the morning newspaper. Mute, Off, Volume — nothing worked. I dialed Maggie, and while the phone rang, I stretched the length of the cord and zeroed the volume on the set.

Maggie answered five or six rings past when voicemail usually picked up. "Sorry, Luv. I was on with Gabby. Her Mikey has a hundred-and-three-degree fever. Have you left?" Her voice sounded like she was in a tunnel.

"No, I'm stuck with another C-section. Are you on the toilet?"

"I'm just giving the little buggers a bath. It's been a day, Bill."

I reclined on the couch while she told me how she had used ice tongs to fish Hot Wheels out of the VCR. Our six- and four-year-olds had used the VCR as a parking garage while they built a mini dirt track on our coffee table. The VCR was ruined, but between what she'd vacuumed up and what our toddler had shoveled into his mouth, you'd never know we'd once had half a bag of potting soil in the family room; now, in the middle of the family room, two loads of clean laundry lay waiting to be folded. I could hear splashing and squealing as she talked. She broke away and threatened "the lot of you" with an extended stay in the Tower of London. They all cheered.

"Maggie, you called me."

"Yes, would you pop into the mini-mart when you're done? Buy some Gatorade and granola bars, the chewy kind, for Ian's match tomorrow. I'm going to switch weeks with Gabby."

"Maggie, please don't go over there. Who knows what

that kid has with all the cats and birds she's got. We don't need you picking up something right now."

"She has two Ragdolls and one African Gray."

"Maggie. Please."

"How was your day? You get any sleep? You sound a bit rough."

"I feel a bit rough. The ladies kept me hopping today."

"Any good girls' names?"

"Maggie, I really don't think that's what we should be doing. Not yet." She became quiet, except for her breathing.

It sounded as if she were cradling the phone to her face. I stepped to the door for a second; the hall was empty.

"Diaz is here. Should I tell him you'll be in for the amnio on Monday?"

She was silent.

"Maggie, if we wait much longer, it will be too late."

"Dr. Diaz said the ultrasound looked fine."

"He also said if we want to know for sure, you need an amnio."

She didn't say anything.

"Listen, we've been over this. Ultrasounds aren't one hundred percent. I showed you the studies."

She cleared her throat. "It's a girl, Luv. It's a girl and she's going to be healthy."

"Maggie, you need to think this through rationally."

"So, what's rational?"

"If the amnio shows forty-six chromosomes, we can relax, pick out a name, and look forward to the delivery."

"If you'd bloody let me, I could do that tonight."

"So, you're fine with taking care of a Down's child for the rest of your life?"

"Oh, that's rational."

"Maggie, all I'm saying is you can't keep ignoring the numbers. Take one hundred women just like you — thirty-nine years old, same blood-test results, same ultrasound — one will have a Down's baby. Sure, only one. But at delivery, if you discover you're that one...well, then, of course, it's way too late."

"Too late?"

"For an abortion."

I wanted to pull back the word abortion as soon as I envisioned it spinning toward her heart. In this my aim was spot on. "I'm not saying we should. But how do you know how you'll feel unless you get the amnio? I mean, for sure."

After a few moments, I heard sniffing, and then a little faraway voice saying, "Mommy's crying. Mommy's crying."

"Maggie, listen, I'm exhausted. You know how I get."

She didn't say anything, and I imagined her sitting on the toilet lid, one hand covering her nose and mouth, her blue eyes gazing at our three little naked boys as they flew their Transformers through the air and plunged them under the water to attack one another.

She spoke softly. "But the handout says one out of two hundred has a miscarriage."

I matched her tone. "It's not even that high. Diaz knows what he's doing."

"This is my last chance, Bill. As you say, what if I'm the one?"

It wasn't that long ago that we had joked about our inability to even conceive a girl. Maggie wondered if I had an X-chromosome in me. Some study her mother sent her claimed that anesthesiologists over in England had boys five to one. Years of breathing trace anesthetic gases, the study postulated. The same study flipped the odds in favor of girls for British fighter pilots. Probably the Gs they pulled. We had two choices, she said: She could hop across the pond and shag a UAF pilot in Brighton, or I could henceforth forsake using inhalation anesthetics and spend some time on the G-Force ride at the Arizona State Fair. In jest I countered that irrespective of X or Y, I hoped my contribution produced a child with twenty digits equally divided among four limbs, a child who could spell color without a "u." That was my hope.

There was a thud and some crying. "Crap, Luke just fell on his bum."

"Maggie."

She cleared her throat again. "I better go. Don't forget the treats."

~

After the C-section, I wheeled Lupe in her bed back to her dimly lit sixth-floor room. Her eyes were closed, and her face cocked to the left over a plastic emesis basin. I slid the chair her mother had been sitting in out of the way, a bouquet of Mylar IT'S A GIRL! balloons tied to the backrest now. The chair settled under the window.

Lightning flickered on the horizon. Taillights edged east along the road leading to my neighborhood in the distant dark. The last mile, wavy with dips, always elicited weightless giggles from the boys. Maggie would be reading a story to them — no doubt *Where the Wild Things Are,* with Ian mouthing the words I'd read to him a hundred times as the boy Max sailed "in and out of weeks and almost over a year."

The nurse applied the blood pressure cuff. Lupe opened an eye, and then vomited the last, the absolute last mouthful (I hoped) of a banana-pudding shake she'd stopped for at Sonic on the way to the hospital. Sometimes, I didn't know what these ladies were thinking.

She spat into the basin. "When can I see my baby?"

"Soon. She's with Antonio in the nursery," the nurse said.

For the ten minutes he had balanced his daughter while she lay on her mother's chest in the C-section room, Antonio kept repeating, she has your nose, she has your nose. I couldn't confirm that it resembled Lupe's nose, but it was beautiful, and it looked normal, as did baby Angelina's eyes, ears, and hands. When the nurse tested Angelina's

Moro reflex, her little arms flung out sideways, as if she had been startled and was reaching for the safety of her mother.

Even after hundreds and hundreds of C-sections, witnessing the shared wonder of young parents often tightened my throat. On this night, while watching Angelina's tiny hand grasp Antonio's finger, my throat tightened a little more, and I had to turn away.

The nurse then guided Antonio toward the door. He carried his squinting daughter as if she were leaking oil; the nurse showed him how to cradle. As the door closed, he held the door with his shoulder and looked back at his wife. His eyes glistened above his mask. "She's so beautiful. She has your nose."

Everyone in the room had laughed — Dr. Diaz running the fascia, his assistant keeping tension on the suture, the scrub nurse finishing up the instrument count — we all laughed as the door thudded shut. Even Lupe. She laughed, she cried, she vomited.

My long day was over. I had the weekend off, but as I strode to the dressing room, I wasn't in a buoyant Friday mood. Since my call to Maggie, it felt like I had a presentation to prepare for Monday.

Then Bonnie stopped me. "Sorry, Doctor. We've got another section."

There it was. She knew that was the best way to tell me. Don't ease it in through the skin, the sub-cue, the muscle; just give it to me sharp and true to the bone.

"First call still busy?" I knew the answer, but it was after nine. I had to try.

"He's still in with the hip," she said. "The femur fractured. They're going to be a while. Second call's busy, too."

I dropped my head, closed my eyes, and clenched. I wanted to say, "No thanks. I'm beat. I can't think. I'm going home." But I didn't. I simply said, "Okay."

"It's room 622," she added. "Diaz just checked her. I gave the Reglan and started pre-loading. The C-section room's turning over." Which meant, *You've got some time to suck it up. I'm going downstairs for a quick smoke.*

Of course, it would have to be the patient who'd asked for the Cadillac treatment, Elizabeth Renke, in 622, the only woman in a ten-mile radius still in labor.

I continued to the doctors' lounge first. I wanted to call Maggie, let her know I'd gotten nailed again and that I might have to pick up the treats in the morning. I shouldn't have mentioned this amnio business earlier, especially over the phone.

A *Cheers* rerun was playing now, the volume still off. It was the season Shelly Long hid behind the counter because in real life she was pregnant. I had always thought the writers missed an opportunity: a pseudo-pregnancy, a largely psychiatric phenomenon. It's bizarre, but it happens. Coffee, which never much appealed to me, felt like a necessity now. But someone had left the burner on. The glass pot was ruined. I slumped into the cushioned chair next to the couch.

I knew I wouldn't turn back the covers until after midnight. And no sleeping in. The boys would be up by six watching cartoons, and Ian's soccer game was at eight. We'd cart everyone out to the park with their blankets and bottles and strollers and Gatorade and still forget one or two things. After our third boy Robbie, I had thought we were done. As much as Maggie wanted to duplicate the photograph she kept at her desk in the bedroom — three-year-old Maggie in a white dress, sitting on a booster chair across from her mother, an elegant setting of flowers, fine china, and cakes between them — we were both creeping toward forty. Our chance of conceiving a Down's baby was increasing exponentially. It was time to count our blessings and move on.

And then one Saturday morning, while I was reading the paper, she pulled a chair close to me. Her hair was wet and combed straight back. She had a sheepish expression. We had made love in the pre-dawn hour before the boys awoke. She put her hand on my wrist and told me that she'd removed her diaphragm in the shower. She said she just wasn't thinking.

"Maggie," I said, "How could you just not be thinking?"

"Oh, you'd rather assume I did it on purpose?"

"I only wish you'd been more careful."

"Look, Luv. It only happened this once. I'm sorry."

Diaz ordered a serum triple-screening test at sixteen weeks. The results indicated Maggie had a one in fifty chance of having a baby with Down's Syndrome compared to one in five hundred for the average woman her age. He recommended an amniocentesis. When Maggie balked, he suggested an ultrasound first. Although we were past the time to detect nuchal thickening, everything else looked clean: none of the bad markers like a hole in the heart's septum or a short femur. And there was one final finding that prompted Maggie to say, "It's the best mistake I ever made." No penis.

But a normal ultrasound can't count chromosomes. It can't tell you if there are forty-seven when there should only be forty-six. Maggie still had a one in a hundred chance. I'd taken care of Down's patients in the OR. I'd seen their problems: the heart defects, the cataracts, periodontal disease. It'd be a lifelong struggle. Was that fair to the child? I'd discussed all this with Maggie.

I picked up the phone and dialed home. The line was busy. I tried to turn up the television volume, but then remembered the remote didn't work. I hurled it to the floor. The plastic cover ejected, and the batteries scattered into hiding.

I phoned again. Still busy. Probably our neighbor Gabby, a perfect name even before her divorce. Why'd Maggie tell her about the ultrasound? It was a short trip from Gabby to her orthopedic surgeon ex-husband to the hospital. I closed my eyes and took two slow breaths, sucking it up before returning to Elizabeth Renke's room.

It had been almost eleven hours since she'd given me the thumbs-up. Her dark hair resembled tangled strands of seaweed. Only a trace of mascara remained as black smears under her closed eyes. Her jaw hung limp. Her legs were spread wide, and her hospital gown, soaked with sweat, was pulled up to her waist while the nurse inserted a bladder catheter. Poor Elizabeth's perineum would be as swollen as an ape's.

When the nurse addressed me, Elizabeth opened her ghastly eyes and offered a weary smile. "I'm sorry."

"What do you mean?" I asked. "Sorry for what?"

"Bonnie said you had to stick around for this."

"Hey, don't say you're sorry. I'd like to know how this story ends."

"I didn't think it'd end this way....Fuck, my last one, too."

Darrel straightened in the corner chair. "Honey!"

"Oh, go back to sleep, Darrel. They'll wake you when they're ready."

Darrel held up his hands in a gesture of surrender. He looked like a referee who had stumbled between two boxers: his hair battered, his white collar unbuttoned, and his pink tie askew.

The nurse straightened Elizabeth's legs and pulled up the sheet.

Elizabeth groaned.

"They turned off the epidural," she said, "to see if I could push better without it. Two fucking hours. There's no fucking way I'd let them do that again."

"Come on, honey. Hold it together just a little longer," Darrel said.

Elizabeth's eyes were closed again, and she laughed the weak, halting laugh of a woman collapsed in the sand a hundred yards from a water hole. "I'm sorry, Darrel. Hard day at the office?"

Darrel laced his fingers and hung his head.

"They also turned off the Pitocin," I said. "That will help."

"Yeah, thank God. Kaylee must have a head as big as a watermelon."

"And stubborn like her mother," Darrel added, not looking up.

"Darrel, will you just shut the fuck up? I'm trying to talk to my doctor here. Why don't you go to the waiting room and tell Mom what's going on? See if she's still got the upper hand with our three little darlings."

As Darrel trudged past me, I grasped his arm. "A nurse will show you where to dress." Then I clapped him on the shoulder. "She'll be fine."

All he could muster was an exhalation, released as if through a trap door.

Elizabeth's behavior wasn't anything I hadn't seen before, and in less than an hour she'd probably be closer to her morning dreamy self than whatever the pain and the hormones and the exhaustion had turned her into now.

In the C-section room, Bonnie and I hooked Elizabeth up to the monitors — blood pressure cuff, ECG, and pulse oximeter. While Bonnie began dosing the epidural, I positioned the oxygen cannula under Elizabeth's nose. It would take several minutes for the numbness to set in, so I broke for the lounge.

On the TV, an anchorwoman with perfect facial features mouthed the ten o'clock news. I plopped into the chair by the phone, dialed, and listened to it ring on the other end. Neighbor Gabby must have run out of gossip for the evening. When Maggie didn't answer, I hung up before the greeting. I tried her cell phone. It went to voicemail immediately. I tried the landline again.

While it was ringing, Darrel walked out of the locker room. He was dressed in scrubs, a cap, and shoe covers. He sat on the couch next to me and said, "The nurse told me to wait here."

I nodded as my voice on the other end of the line said *please leave a message.* "Maggie, can you hear me? Pick up. It's 10:05. Do you know where your wife is? I mean, where my wife is. You know what I mean." It pissed me off that she wouldn't pick up, and I thought, well fuck her. She can just lay there and worry about me until I get home.

Darrel was staring at me with the same weary indifference that I was trying to hide from him, so I finished my message to Maggie with, "I'm sure you've got a good explanation. You usually do."

For Darrel's sake, I smiled and shook my head, as if to say, there's no accounting for women.

After hanging up, I asked, "Have you seen Dr. Diaz?"

Darrel angled his head toward the locker room. "He's gowning up."

Emerging from the dressing room, Diaz tied his wedding ring into the bow on his scrub pants and hiked the waist after he was done. "Man, I need a little less belly or a little more butt." He clapped his hands. "Okay, let's do it." Then he paused and looked at me. "How many girls does this make for you?"

"Ten."

Darrel looked puzzled.

I said, "All my patients today have had girls. If you want a girl, I seem to have a pink thumb. At least, today."

Darrell took a deep breath and clasped his hands behind his head. "Anything, Doc. Anything. Just get this baby delivered."

Diaz laughed. "Man, this is the easy part. In sixteen years when your little girl wants a car for her birthday, that's when it's tough. You know where you'll be when she bats her eyes and says, 'All my friends have new cars?'"

"No."

Diaz held out his little finger. "Wrapped right here."

Darrel dropped his hands to his lap and smiled, the first time I'd seen him smile since morning. His bouncy-hearted dream was back on track and chugging toward a day when he'd hand his daughter the keys and feel rich being wrapped around her perfect little finger.

In the C-section room, Elizabeth lay slightly tilted to the left in a modified crucifix position. A blue drape rose from her chest, secured to IV stands positioned near the extended arm-boards. Her arms had been secured loosely to the boards with Velcro straps, a reminder not to touch her belly during the prep. I released the straps. Diaz, his nurse first-assistant, and the scrub nurse stood at the table. They were arranging the last few things: raising the instrument tray over Elizabeth's numb and draped legs, throwing one end of the sterile suction tubing to the circulating nurse, and wiping the talc from their gloves with a saline-soaked lap.

Diaz said, "Kelly."

The nurse snapped a Kelly clamp into his palm.

He pinched Elizabeth's skin where he wanted to make the incision and said, "Liz, do you feel that?"

"Feel what?" she asked.

"How about here?" He pinched as far north on her abdomen as was exposed by the rectangular opening in the drape.

"Are you doing something?" she said.

Bonnie headed out the door.

I leaned close to Elizabeth's ear. "He's just testing to see if you're numb." I had already checked her, lightly marching an eighteen-gauge needle up the middle of her chest until she felt a pinprick. I straightened up and looked over the drape. "She's good."

Diaz handed the Kelly back. "All right, another miracle by the good doctor. Let's do it. Knife please." He palpated her abdomen with his left hand and accepted the scalpel in his right. Then he stopped and looked up. "Oh, how about the father?"

"He's on the way," I said.

A moment later, Bonnie opened the door and Darrel walked in.

She said, "I'm going to check the board."

I nodded and patted the rolling stool positioned by Elizabeth's head. Darrel took his seat behind the drape. He grasped his wife's outstretched hand and kissed it through his mask. "This is it," he said.

Elizabeth was the only one in the room who wasn't wearing a mask. She turned her head toward him and gave a weak smile. Darrel plucked a tissue from the box on my anesthesia cart and wiped her eyes. She looked back toward the ceiling, her gaze roaming left and right. "Have they started?"

"We're on our way," I said.

Diaz took less than two minutes from skin down to the uterus. All Elizabeth could know, and Darrel for that matter since he didn't stand, was what could be heard. Instruments snapped smartly in latex gloves. Air hissed through the suction wand until there was the sharp slurping of blood being cleared from the surgical field. Clamps closed with a crisp crunch of their ratchets.

Elizabeth's eyes continued to search the room. "What are they doing now?"

Before I could answer, there was a gush of fluid onto the floor. "What, what was that?"

"This is where it feels like someone is sitting on your chest," I said.

The nurse assistant leaned her face over the drape and spoke to Elizabeth. "Sorry about this." And then she pressed her forearm and opposite hand into Elizabeth's upper abdomen and drove all that was inside toward Diaz's waiting hand.

As the head popped into the world through the open incision, Elizabeth groaned. "Oh, what was that?"

"That's Kaylee Ann taking a peek," I said. "Dr. Diaz is suctioning her mouth."

"Is she okay? I don't hear anything. Is she okay? Is she okay, Darrel?"

"Should I look?" Darrel asked. "Is it okay to look?"

"She's fine," I said.

"Can I stand up?"

"Sure," I said to Darrel. "Go ahead. Stand up."

As if he were about to catch a first glimpse of an undiscovered land, Darrel stood. He kept hold of his wife's hand, never quite pushing the stool back. "Honey, I see her head."

The nurse assistant leaned over and compressed Elizabeth's stomach. "One more push. Sorry."

The baby slid from the womb into Diaz's hands and immediately began to wail.

"I see her, I see her, honey." Darrel pulled his mask down and kissed his wife. She was sobbing now and their tears mixed and I thought to tell him later if the chance arose: *I told you she'd be fine.*

The circulator looked at the clock on the wall. "Ten thirty-six." I nodded and jotted the time on my record.

"All right," Diaz said. "There you go. This is one kid that was too big for the chute."

The nurse began drying the baby with a small blue towel, wiping nature's white packing grease from the face while Diaz clamped and cut the cord. "Pitocin please," he said.

I was injecting the amp of Pit into the IV bag when he said, "Hey... Elizabeth."

Darrel looked over at Diaz.

"What?" she said, wiping her nose with a tissue. "Is something wrong? Can I see her? When can I see her?"

"Did you buy a lot of pink baby clothes?" Diaz said.

"Well, yeah, I guess," she said.

"I'm afraid he was hiding something from us, my dear."

"What? I don't understand....Darrel?"

Diaz faced the baby toward Darrel for a moment, and then handed him off to the nurse by the warmer.

"It's a boy, Lizzy," Darrel said. "Oh, my God. It's okay, Lizzy, it's a healthy boy." He looked back at Diaz. "He's healthy, right?"

The baby cried and punched the cool air with his arms and legs. I pictured his lungs expanding to their full rosy capacity.

Diaz was easing the placenta free. "He looks great. I'm betting he tops ten pounds."

"You can go see him if you want," I said.

Darrel's look questioned me and I repeated, "Go ahead."

He looked down at Elizabeth. Her eyes were closed, her tears gone.

"I'm going to see our son," he said. "Liz?"

She jerked her hand away and made a fist on her chest.

"I'll be right back," he said, stepping over to the radiant warmer and looking down at his son.

"Elizabeth," I said. "Are you feeling okay?"

She didn't answer for a few seconds, and then inhaled deeply. "No," she said, her pitch rising on the exhalation.

"Are you feeling any pain?"

She didn't answer.

Diaz was stitching her up.

"Is that tugging bothering you?" I said.

She opened her eyes and fixed them on the ceiling.

"We've got about twenty, twenty-five minutes to go," I said. "Let me know if you need anything. Elizabeth?...Elizabeth?"

"I thought the ultrasound said it was a girl." She said this loud enough for Diaz to hear. And then louder, "I thought you fucking said it was a girl."

There was silence — except for the monitors, except for the baby.

He cried.

We looked at one another, all but Elizabeth, our shocked expressions eventually settling on Dr. Diaz.

His hands running on muscle memory, he stared just past the suture he was tying.

"Ultrasounds aren't a hundred percent," he said. "We talked about that, Elizabeth. Nothing is one hundred percent."

"I don't care. I don't want a boy. I...want...my...girl."

The ECG monitor seemed to beep louder than I'd ever heard it in the C-section room. I was never so conscious of a mother's heart rate. It was the baby's heart rate we all listened to on obstetrics. And after a baby delivered, after he cried his heart out for his mother, after we knew he was safely on his way in the world, we stopped listening and talked about other things. But now, no one talked about what movies they were going to see this weekend, or their kids' soccer games, or their pregnant wives.

At the warmer, Darrel doted on his son, stroking the back of the boy's tiny hand, while the nurse placed a band around the infant's ankle. She patted Darrel's arm, whispering something I couldn't hear. He nodded and forced a smile. The baby was quiet now, wrapped tight in a blanket and with a stocking cap covering his pointy head.

Darrel scooped up his son, and I steadied the stool while he sat. He looked at the solemn, sleeping face of the boy. "Honey?...We could call him Kyle."

She turned her head away. "I don't want to see it."

He leaned the baby's head onto her shoulder. "Liz, don't be silly."

She yanked her shoulder away. "Darrel! I said I don't want to see it. I want my girl."

"Liz. That's not fair." He said this with a gentle yet firm tone, a tone I'd heard from Maggie.

"You're right," she said. "It's not fair."

Darrel looked up at me, then down at his son, and back to me. His eyes, squinting above his mask, pleaded for an explanation: How could she act like this? How could she not embrace her child? But I had never seen this before. I had no rational answer; not as a doctor, or a husband, or a father.

"There's no excuse for this, Liz," he said. "No excuse." And then, carrying his bewilderment and his child close to his chest, he followed the nurse out the door.

I sat behind Elizabeth's icy expression, not knowing what to say. Listening was all I could do, and what I heard was the ECG machine transducing the beat of her heart into a sound that was sterile and foreign.

"Elizabeth, do you need anything?" I asked.

Again, she was quiet.

"Let me know if you start to feel queasy...Elizabeth? Listen, I can't help you if you don't talk to me." I turned away and ripped the packaging from a bag of saline. I laid the liter bag on my workspace, and then drew an amp of Pitocin into a syringe.

"I don't need your fucking help," she said. "I need my girl."

I turned to her.

She arched her head back so she could glare at me. "You got one of those back there with all your stuff?"

I didn't respond.

She lay back down. "I should have just gotten an abortion. Darrel didn't think we could afford a fourth kid anyway."

My heartbeat, charged with anger and a kind of fear I'd never felt in an operating room, leapt into my throat, my ears, and the tips of my fingers. As I tried to inject Pitocin into the saline bag's port, the needle shook. I stopped and in a voice loud enough to merit a glance from Diaz, said, "You're very lucky, you know."

She arched again to peer at me. "Oh, am I?"

I pointed the syringe and needle at her. My hand trembled. "Damn right you are."

"I hear you're the lucky one." She smiled in a smug way, as if she were privy to a secret, as if by looking at me upside down, she'd found an angle into my soul. "Yeah, Bonnie told me you're having a girl. Want to switch?"

"Sure, maybe I will!" I said, my voice quaking. "You know, there's a chance she might — !" I choked off the rest. I raised the syringe above my head and plunged the needle into the bag of saline, as if driving it into the heart of a beast.

Elizabeth flinched and then her expression steadied. "She might what?" she said. "Be a boy?"

I dropped Elizabeth off in her room, and then spoke briefly with Diaz in the lounge. I apologized for my outburst. He waved it off, saying the whole case was filled with antics he'd never seen before. When he told me he'd ordered a psych consult for her, I thought, he should have ordered one for me as well.

It was past midnight. I didn't bother to change out of my scrubs, but wadded up my clothes and tossed them into the passenger seat of the MG. I put the top down. A thunderstorm had passed through, and the aroma of desert creosote curled over the windshield as I steered eastward along the wet, empty streets.

At a stoplight, the phone rang. Maggie's ID came up. Two hours prior, I would have let it ring. "Luv, that was a bloody long C-section," she said. "You coming home?"

"I had another. Why didn't you answer my call?"

The light turned green.

"You called?" she said.

I switched the phone to speaker, rested the handset on my lap, and powered through the gears.

"That must have been while I was outside," she said. "You won't believe the night I've had."

The phone had the hollow sound of an overseas call.

Maggie explained how she was reading *Where the Wild Things Are* to the boys when Gabby phoned. And when she went back to their room, Ian wasn't in bed and he wasn't in the bathroom. So she looked in the swimming pool first and then called his name throughout the house, and he didn't answer. She went out front and was shouting his name so loudly that the neighbors started coming outside, which must have been when I phoned. Gabby wanted to call the police, but Maggie went inside to call me first, and when I didn't answer, she knew I was with a patient. That's when she noticed a little tuft of red hair poking out of the clean laundry piled in the middle of the family room.

"He's asleep," she said. "I left him there. You have to

see him. I could blister his bum, that little bugger, but he looks so cute."

She finished with what sounded to me like a cleansing breath. "So, Luv, how'd your sections go?"

I could have told her about Elizabeth, how she shunned her baby and I lost my cool. I could have pointed out that Elizabeth's ultrasound was wrong and then regurgitated the statistics. I was full of statistics. But what was the chance a mother or a father couldn't love their child if she wasn't what they'd hoped for? One out of a hundred? One out of a million? Who was the one?

I knew it wasn't Maggie. At least I had that. I was silent. The dips in the road were flooded, and I was struggling to keep a connection.

"Bill, you there?" Maggie called into the night.

I took the phone off speaker, pulling her voice close to my ear. "I'm here."

"You okay, Luv. Is everything okay?"

"I hope," I said. "I hope."

PART III

THE LATER YEARS

A TRIBUTE TO CHAPSTICK

PROSE POEM

My waxy guardian expired today. I will remember his bullet posture, his taut black suit with the red lapels, the white derby hat secured tight to his head with a crisp snap. A staid visage indeed compared to the saucy lads dressed in raspberry and pumped with PABA. He retained the little circle R after his name, a reminder of his royal legacy, which softened the indignity of long hours deep in my trousers' pocket. There he waited in stoic silence. Not even my curvaceous keys or charismatic coins could entice him to spin his tiny wheel. Yet, on occasion, at night he'd steal to the laundry room where I'd find him the next morning, giddy and tumbled dry.

But when called to serve, he deflects sun and wind; moisturizing my lips, soothing my chafed confidence.

He offered relief one invisible layer at a time until all that remained was his hollow tube and the lingering aroma of eucalyptus and camphor — the fragrance of an unheralded healing life.

COMPS

Saturday morning and George, shifting his weight from one leg to the other, stood in line at Starbucks. There were still four customers ahead of him. At one point he folded his arms and sighed — the puffy-cheeked, trumpeter sigh that bugged his wife Annie. Just thirty minutes ago she'd said *must you do that* as he chauffeured her to the airport. She was forever running off on weekends. This time to Oklahoma City for another site visit at that big casino project. He sighed again. At the front of the line, a bemused elderly couple fumbled over their order. Snowbirds no doubt. The pumpkin spice latte had them stumped.

George muttered, "Geez, don't they have Starbucks in Iowa?"

The woman directly in front of George turned her owlish face to his and glowered. Pretending to read the menu on the wall, he stuffed his hands in his sports coat pockets and fired a stealth double bird.

He needed to calm down. That had been his plan coming in here. Buy a paper or begin the book Annie had left on the seat in her rush to escape the car, and then, once suitably decompressed, head home to tackle the irrigation valve that had gone kaput. On the west side of their house, a stand of Eldarica Pines, forty-foot testaments to a dozen family Christmases past, were dying: drooping branches, brown needles, bark flaking off. They'd probably not had water for months, maybe years. Who knew? Landscapers came and went. They were all worthless. Annie hadn't noticed the trees, not with her schedule. And George? He had his own deadlines — Boeing, Hughes, it didn't matter. All his clients wanted the drawings yesterday. It took a dying branch unloading its weight on the roof and the crash of a couple of cement tiles to draw George to the trees. He investigated. No water. Not a good thing in Arizona.

If he was lucky it would just be a burned-out solenoid. A simple exchange. But he didn't feel lucky. Oh no, the problem wouldn't be clear-cut — maybe a bad O-ring, maybe a leaky diaphragm — and in any case, he'd have to cut out the whole valve. That meant digging a four-foot-diameter hole to allow enough play in the piping to install the new unit. He figured by five o'clock he would have put in six hours of work, made three trips to the specialty plumbing store, and still have a vast hole in the ground, a valve that wouldn't fit, and no time to fix the fricking mess until next weekend. Of course, Annie would find a way to use this the next time they argued about selling the house.

"The usual, Mr. B?"

"Yes, Kim," George said.

She keyed the register as she recited, "Grande nonfat cappuccino, heavy on the foam." She looked up. "Anything else?"

"No, thanks." He handed her his gold Starbucks card and then stepped over to the pickup counter.

After eighteen years in the same house, Annie wanted to downsize. They'd discussed it again on the drive to the airport this morning. She turned off the radio, silencing the local home-improvement call-in show, and then laid out her arguments. It was a speech he'd heard a few times: the younger of their two boys was now in college, the comparable home values looked promising, and the market was sizzling. If they were going to sell, this was the perfect opportunity.

He kept his eyes on the road and deflected her points one by one as best he could. The debate continued for several minutes. The financials were on her side, and he could feel her gaining momentum, driving him into a corner. He realized he was squeezing the steering wheel; his grip pulsed on the burnished leather.

Annie noticed. "You don't have to get angry, George."

"Dammit, Annie," he'd said. "I'm happy where we live. I don't need — or want — a new house." He immediately regretted shouting.

She became quiet and stared out the side window. The freeway passed over the Salt River. They bumped along the bridge's expansion joints, the clapping tires and squeaky center console the only sounds in the car.

She raised the temperature a degree and adjusted the vents. George was already burning up. Then he caught a whiff of her perfume, his favorite, and he had the urge to reach over and stroke the rim of her ear. But the aroma lingered for only a second and was gone.

A few miles later, she said, "George, you never feel like it's time for a change, do you." Her voice was restrained and desolate. He glanced her way. She was still looking out the window.

"What do you mean?"

"The same old house, the same old car, the same week in San Diego every summer...our lives just plod along. Don't you *ever* get bored? Don't you ever want to try something different?"

George took a deep breath. She was never satisfied. "So, we're back to that. Change for change's sake?"

She turned slowly. "No, George. Not change for change's sake. Change to make something better." Sometimes, she got this look where she half-smiled, bobbed her head, and raised her eyebrows. It made him feel like he had butter for brains. He didn't turn his head, but he knew she was giving him that look.

When he stopped at the airport, she just shook her head and said, "You are so predictable."

"Hey, there's nothing wrong with that."

"George, I'm serious about this."

"Well, I'm serious, too."

"Look, we'll talk about it when I get back."

"When's that again?"

"Stop it."

They kissed like foreign diplomats, and then she hustled toward curbside check-in. She wore her new olive skirt suit. Her stride was unmistakable, almost like a brisk walk across a tightrope. Her calves were her fingerprint — one in a million. Their firm contours had always reminded him of mirrored treble clefs. He could practically trace his life by the moments he'd watched them flex: during college as she ran past him during a touch football game on a northern California beach; as she patiently taught their oldest a forehand stroke using a pint-sized racket; as they dashed up eight flights of stairs in their hotel moments after the Loma Prieta earthquake to get her purse (that seemed foolish now); a couple years later, during his hospitalization for kidney stones, as she tiptoed out of his room around midnight — way past visiting hours. She'd paused at his hospital room door, turned, and given him a look full of promise and affection. Just for him. The best medicine.

Look back, he thought after she'd checked her bag and approached the automatic glass doors. *Look back like you did then.*

His car idling, he waited, but when the doors opened, she strode through and was gone. God, Annie pissed him off sometimes.

George prepared his drink at the small stand of sugars and stirrers and napkins. On a busy day like today, the line of customers waiting to order crowded the stand. It was an inefficient use of space, and he'd mentioned this once to Annie, ergonomics being something he dealt with at work.

"Don't stress, George," she said. "Starbucks has a certain way of doing things." Like she couldn't take the time to hear him out.

He removed the lid and set it on the counter, sharp edge down. He aligned two sugar packets, gave them a single brisk shake, and tore the ends off simultaneously. A woman reached around him.

George glanced at her. She wore oversized, deep-tinted sunglasses, and as she plucked a second napkin, her attention seemed to be on the dispenser.

"I'm sorry," he said as he took a step aside, reaching for his coffee and the lid.

"No, no. Don't move. You're perfect."

"Can I get that in writing?" George asked, smiling. She laughed and acknowledged him with a return smile before moving away.

I'd like to show my wife, he thought, and poured the sugar in the center of the latte's foam. He counted out three wooden stir sticks, whipped the sugar to the bottom, and replaced the lid, taking care to feel the final snap.

George surveyed the crowded room. As usual, the wiry, bearded cowboy with his hat cocked forward sat hunkered over a chess set and an open book. Three bicyclists in team colors clacked over to one of two vacant tables. The other empty table was near a klatch of ladies he'd seen here on and off the past few months scribbling god knows what on their yellow pads and yucking it up. Then he spied a faux leather club chair by the window, the only cushioned seat left. The chair shared a small side table with the woman who said he was perfect.

She had removed her sunglasses and began writing in a thick daytimer. When he sat down she didn't look up. He guessed she was ten years younger than he, more or less, and in good shape. She wore a leopard-skin blouse, something Annie would have mocked, but it went well with her black skirt and sweater. She seemed a little slimmer than Annie.

Maybe a little taller. It wouldn't surprise him if she'd once played on her college tennis team as Annie had. He thought about allowing his coffee to cool by removing the lid, but decided to be safe and accept a slightly burned tongue (if it came to that) rather than risk spilling the full cup. For the moment, at least, one beautiful woman thought he was perfect, and he didn't want to tarnish that image.

He put on his reading glasses, crossed his legs, and flipped through the book. It was a collection of short stories Annie had bought him about a year ago. He guessed she'd hoped to extend his literary sensibility beyond history, particularly Civil War history. He no longer remembered exactly how the gift had turned into an argument, but it had, and the book ended up on her shelf.

"They make this coffee so hot," the woman said, causing George to look over his glasses. "It's forever before I can start drinking it."

She held a Venti-sized takeout cup in one hand and waved her other hand in front of her mouth, her lips forming the letter "O."

"I know what you mean," he said. "I should have taken the lid off mine."

She blew lightly across the top of her cup, sending steam in his direction. There was a slight peak to her glossy upper lip, and from the vermilion edge a small parenthesis-shaped scar flexed under her makeup. Her hair was auburn (dyed perhaps) and thicker than Annie's natural brunette. George liked the way her loose curls corkscrewed to her shoulders. This was a style that Annie should try. Isn't that what she was always asking of him? Try something new.

"I've never been to this Starbucks." The woman looked around. "Is it always this crowded?"

"It is this time of day."

George returned to his book, then paused, took off his reading glasses, and grinned.

"Excuse me. I'm curious."

"Yes."

"How do you know this isn't *my* first time here?"

"Oh, I don't know. I just assumed." She eyed him. "You have a look."

"How's that?"

"It's hard to say. Maybe the way you're dressed — a sports coat with jeans, the crew neck shirt. Maybe the way you walk, the way you hold your cup." With her palm, she traced a circle as if she were casting a spell. "You put it all together, and it just seems to me you've been here before."

That was a stretch, and had Annie said it, he would have blasted her, but he relished the woman's attention. It felt like a compliment. He sat up a little straighter.

"The book, too," she said.

"This?" He held the book up.

"A man doesn't carry a book unless he's going someplace to read."

"Maybe I've been there and stopped by Starbucks on my way home."

"You mean your favorite neighborhood Starbucks?"

"Very good."

"I can read people," she said with a tilt to her head. "So what's it called?"

He examined the book's cover. "*Mendocino.*"

"Never heard of it."

"Doesn't surprise me. It's a book of short stories. My wife gave it to me."

"How do *you* know I don't like short stories?" She grinned.

"I assumed you wouldn't."

"I wasn't talking about the book. I meant the place. Where is it?"

"Mendocino? In California. I can't picture where, though."

"So, here's a question for you. How do people choose a book?"

"By the cover?"

"And how do people choose their agent? They look online and pick the face they like. In my experience, you George Clooney types scoop up all the women clients... the gay men, too."

George had never thought of himself as resembling George Clooney. Handsome enough to have attracted

Annie, yes, but no Clooney except for maybe the hair. He did have Clooney's hair, equally gray. Annie used to twirl George's hair at his collar. But that was years ago when he'd worn it longer.

The woman's cell phone rang — a riff he hadn't heard before — daring, optimistic notes racing up the neck of a steel-string guitar. She answered and, while listening, curled her lower lip under her upper teeth. He lingered on her eyes as they wandered. She wore very little makeup, much like Annie. Then it came to him — *mother-of-pearl inlay*. That's what her eyes reminded him of, and not the whitish sort of inlay on guitars but more opal in color. She crossed her legs and let a pump dangle from her toes, a seductive gesture directed at him, George thought.

"That's okay. You come down the 60 and exit at Dobson," she said into the phone. She shifted and winked at George. He smiled and noticed she wasn't wearing a wedding ring. Noticed? He'd looked for it and was conscious of his own. Then a shadowy thought darted past the tapered edge of his mind's light — a kind of drive-by thought: *I wish she didn't know I was married.*

"You'll have to do a U-turn and come back to it...no... no problem. I'll see you in thirty." She hung up, and then while smiling, rolled her eyes and said, "Clients. Californians. They were almost to Florence. I'm meeting them here." She opened her appointment book and jotted a note. She didn't seem irritated that her clients were late.

Annie would have blown up if an architect or builder kept her waiting. However, this lovely woman smiled and then moved her chair — and her interest in him — a little closer. He reminded himself that she'd started this conversation, and he was merely following along.

"Look, I'm going to be here another thirty minutes," she said. "I must be keeping you from something."

"Yes, you are," he said. "An afternoon of hard labor. I'm George." He offered his hand. "The name is all I have in common with Mr. Clooney."

She laughed and shook his hand. "I'm Cathie." She flipped open her stout daytimer and pulled a card from the inside pocket. "In case you ever need an agent."

George accepted the card. She worked for a major outfit. He sipped his coffee. It was down to the last quarter cup and cold.

"You need a refill?" He gestured to her cup. "That'd be perfect." She reached for her handbag.

"No, no. My treat," he said. "What are you having?"

"Surprise me."

George ordered two cappuccinos and a pumpkin scone. He told Kim to use ceramic cups and not too hot this time. Lattes always charged him with confidence, invincibility even. He was feeling it. And something else. When he returned from the restroom, his order was ready.

He asked Cathie if she'd like to split the scone. She said she'd love to. He cut it at the table they shared and offered her the larger half. She turned it around and gave it to him.

"I've got to confess," she said.

George met her eyes, and he tried to appear nonchalant while musing over possible confessions he thought — even guiltily hoped — she might make. *I hope my clients never show. I don't usually flirt with married men. I was hoping you'd ask me to dinner tonight.*

"That whole thing about your clothes and the book and being a regular? Not entirely true. I heard you order your drink. The girl at the counter knew you."

His heart downshifted a gear.

"Still, that's very good," he said. "And as long as we're confessing, I'm not really perfect."

She threw her head back but then cut short her laugh, seemingly embarrassed by her sudden outburst. George liked that about her, not her sense of decorum, but her unabashed validation of his joke. He couldn't remember the last time Annie laughed like that.

"Oh, don't sell yourself short, George." She touched his arm again. "I'll bet you're closer to perfect than you think."

As their conversation continued, George sipped his cappuccino (the temperature was perfect) and ate his half of their scone. He learned she'd been a real estate agent for twelve years. She'd gone to college in Tucson, dropped out halfway to a psychology degree, and then moved to Phoenix with her boyfriend Cliff. That led to marriage.

They never had kids (she didn't say why) but it was a good thing because they divorced a couple years ago. Cliff couldn't handle her success, as she put it. He ran a produce company. She'd dated a little since, even tried speed dating once, although no long-term prospects emerged.

That didn't matter. Things had really taken off for her. Eighteen-hour days, but she wasn't complaining. If you wanted to get ahead, you had to put in the work. "No pain, no gain," she said — a cliché George normally hated, but not today.

For his part George threw his dying trees, his lifelong love of music, and eventually his frayed marriage into the growing stack of life's intimate details accumulating between them. He told her he was a product designer. He led her through college and then grad school in the Bay Area, those first jobs designing Rollerblades and snow-boards, his facility with computer-aided design that had prepared him for his current position as lead designer for a Scottsdale company. He'd worked on everything from cockpits of helicopters to overhead storage on jumbo jets. He was boasting, sure, but it felt great. For the last couple years, he'd played trumpet in a garage band on Tuesday nights.

"Dixieland Jazz," he said.

"Like 'When the Saints Go Marching In'?"

"Yes. My wife's not a fan."

"Not my favorite either, I'm afraid."

"But if I had a street-fair gig, you'd show up? Right?"

"Absolutely," she said. "Long as I wasn't showing a house." She winked. "What else?"

She leaned forward and he floated on her creamy expression, especially when she pursed her lips and blew over the top of her cup. He imagined kissing her along the pale scar of her upper lip, soft and tenderly as if playing a ballad. He wanted to feel the buzz again.

He told her his wife, a structural engineer, traveled more frequently now that the boys were building their own lives out of state. He was lucky to see her four days out of seven. George watched Cathie closely. She was listening with an expression of concern. He admitted he didn't always do the things Annie wanted him to. He hated plays, particularly musicals, so Annie usually went with a friend. They differed on other things, and he rattled off a few of them, from his preference not to trade out of their San Diego timeshare (Cathie interjected she loved San Diego) to choice of yogurt. He could have gone on but didn't. The list of ways Annie and he differed now seemed endless — or, if not endless, then longer than it used to be.

"Dannon versus Yoplait was like the battle at Antietam," he said.

They laughed and she added, "At least it wasn't as bad as Gettysburg."

"No, it wasn't," he said, marveling at her retort.

For a moment they were silent. George sensed she was waiting for him to take the lead.

"You know the worst thing?" he said.

"Tell me."

"Anymore, she's in bed by nine and out the door by five-thirty." He sipped the last of his cappuccino. "It's tough."

"Cliff and I were the same way. Ships passing in the night," she said. "There were things I missed." And then she brought the cup to her lips, pointed her blue-inlay eyes at him, and, with a wan smile, added, "Still are."

Elbows on his knees, George leaned forward and thumbed her card, his pulse pounding as he stroked the embossed letters. Certainly, she was making him an offer. She would sleep with him if he wanted, but he sensed something more in her sad smile, something just beyond his grasp.

"I really need to redo that photo," she said softly.

"No, the photo's fine," he said. "Interesting spelling of your first name."

"I didn't like it so much when I was younger. It was different from the way 'Cathy' is normally spelled, but it kind of fits the way I am now."

George wanted to ask, How different are you now from when you were younger? Different enough to give a married man a spec house tour and then make love to him in the plush-carpeted master bedroom? It would be love, wouldn't it? It would be more than sex. The glow would last more than a day, an hour, a minute. Years from now, you'd remember you once said he was perfect.

"My wife thinks we should sell our house and get something smaller."

"Where do you live?" she asked.

"Around the corner." It surprised him this hadn't come up yet.

"You should think about it. The market's not going to stay this hot forever. If you want, I could run the comps in your area so you can see what you're missing."

He thought for a moment, but not about whether to sell the house.

"Will your wife be home?" she added.

"No," he said. "She's gone for the weekend."

"What are you doing later today?"

"I should deal with my trees."

"Maybe tonight?" She put a hand on George's knee and leaned in.

With very little effort he could kiss her lips.

"Tonight?" He rubbed the card, Annie's challenge in his ears — *You never change. You're so predictable.* His heart pounded.

"I'll bring dinner," she said. "From Tía Rosa's. Have you eaten there?"

"No."

"Oh, it's great. Cliff used to take me there every Wednesday for lunch. We loved how they season their pork. And the margaritas? The best. He always kidded me when I ordered mine with half the ice."

She was charged, effusive, and George now knew what he'd seen in her smile. Cathie missed Cliff, or at least their best times, their companionable moments. George looked around. He realized he'd lost track of the bustle at Starbucks. The bicyclists had left, replaced by a man and woman new to George. But the cowboy still strategized over his chess set. The dear ladies leaned in toward the center of their table and whispered something before pulling back into an uproarious laugh.

"No, Cathie, I'm afraid I can't."

"Sunday, then."

"Look, Annie and I are going to talk about the house when she gets home."

She sat back in her chair. He wasn't sure what she would do. He fiddled with her card.

She took it back and stared at it for several seconds. "George, be honest." She leaned forward and held out the card.

He took it.

"Let's say you *were* in the market to sell your house. And let's say you didn't know me, and you needed an agent. If all you had was this picture to go by, would you choose me?"

He studied the card once more. The only blemish was the scar.

"Cathie," he said, looking straight into her eyes, "the photo looks great. *You* look great."

"Thanks," she said. "You're sweet." She placed her phone and daytimer on the chair. "Watch my things a moment, will you?"

"Sure," he said. "Oh, sure."

The phone wasn't about to run away, but still, what she might be worried about was another customer slipping it in their pocket and scooting out the door. So he did what he had promised. As always, Mr. Reliable.

Let's see. Dinner, she'd said, and she would provide. In the time between now and then, he could make a run by the hardware store for parts. With luck he'd be home by four. He'd have time to run the dishwasher and take a shower.

Heels clicking across the floor, Cathie returned. Her phone buzzed and the screen lit up, message coming in. Frowning, she gave him the briefest of glances. "You should have answered."

"What — ?"

"But, it's okay. It's a text, not a call." Still standing, she read it. "Oh, damn. My clients are in the parking lot. Maybe we should postpone."

"Uh, okay."

"Thanks for filling the time." She reached out for his hand and pumped it. "And if you ever get serious about selling your place, you know where to find me."

Did he?

She gathered her things and moved away in clipped steps, past the cowboy and the ladies, past the pick-up counter and the service stand, and out into the Saturday sunshine.

He looked down at the card. C-A-T-H-I-E. An odd spelling after all.

Drumming his fingers, he waited at the counter of the plumbing specialty shop. Expletives ran like a ticker tape through his brain, but you couldn't say those words now, or women would kill you.

The owner's son, a college kid who worked there on Saturdays, dropped the parts on the counter. "Here you go," he said. "Will there be anything else?"

"Just ring me up," George snapped.

"Is something the matter?"

"Nothing," he said, at least nothing he could put his finger on. Nine times out of ten, a plumbing repair required a second trip.

He brought home a solenoid and complete valve set and changed into his favorite old jeans and work shirt. Of course, the solenoid wasn't the problem and the valve set was a whole different model, but by god it would fit and he only had to return to the specialty shop once for more pipe glue and 45-degree adaptors. He still had to dig that big four-foot-diameter hole he'd been dreading, but he took his time and went at it with an eye to the trees and the shade they provided on the west side of the house.

As he dug, George thought again of his conversation with Annie in the car that morning. She claimed he feared change. But it wasn't change he feared — he feared regret, the second thoughts that come after the deed is done. He'd told her something to that effect.

"Annie," he'd said. "I like our house. I know its quirks. There's nothing out there I'd feel as comfortable in."

"But you'll never know unless you look around," she said.

"Let's say you look around," he said. "Weekend after weekend until one day a house seems to speak to you. You fall in love with it. The vaulted ceilings, the stainless-steel appliances, the carpet thick and soft and smelling like move-in day. Then after a while you notice the cracks and the leaks. The closets that you thought workable now seem too small. You'd wonder why you ever moved. Can't you see that?"

"Yes, I can, George," she'd said. "But I'll take my chances."

Of course, she would. They differed that way. Now he wondered if she'd been trying to tell him something, maybe one of her own drive-by thoughts venturing into brighter light. That's what scared him as he dug, as he repaired the valve, as sweat stung his eyes, as *their* earth — Annie's and his — collected under his nails, as the sun settled behind *their* trees, as he turned *their* water back on and watched it soak into *their* ground.

George leaned on the shovel. Weary and proud, but hopeful in the dying light of this day, he envisioned the water coursing through the trees' limbs, plumping them back to life, greening the needles after so many neglected months. If these tired and withered pines could come back, then so could he and Annie.

He liked this house, he loved this house, but he didn't need it. What he needed couldn't be found with a beguiling stranger in a Starbucks. When Annie came home, he would tell her everything, and together maybe they could find a real estate agent who could help them with some comps.

BAGGAGE CLAIM

Weary holiday travelers clustered around the carousels at Sky Harbor's baggage claim. A cold front had swept down from the Northwest, delaying flights all Christmas Eve day and into the night. Every few minutes an announcement stirred the mass of travelers. A bell sounded, hands pointed to a red beacon flashing above one carousel or another, and a few passengers, drawn by the bell and the beacon, aligned anew. In the middle of one such display, a man, wearing a Levi's jacket over a gaily colored sweater, emerged from the men's room. With a slight hitch to his step, he negotiated the crowd, angling toward carousel five. On the far side stood a woman. She wore a bulky shearling coat with a stain on the sleeve. The woman gave the man a hard look as he approached. She maintained that look even after she handed him a weathered, leather satchel and even after he looped the satchel's broad strap across his chest and struck a parade-rest posture beside her.

"So? How is it?" she asked.

"It's fine. I told you, dear, I'm fine." He scanned the few remaining pieces of luggage as they circled by, shook his head, and said, "Damn coffee. I never should have had more coffee in Denver."

"It's not the coffee," the woman said.

She gazed at him for several seconds while the man continued to follow the bags. Finally, she pushed up her coat's sleeve and tapped her watch. "Well, I'm going to talk to somebody," she said. "Thirty-five minutes. This is ridiculous."

"Give it a little longer," he said. "Everyone's waiting. Everyone's bags are late. They'll come."

"You'd think the airline could plan," she said. "Look at the calendar. They should know. Sweet Jesus, a little foresight. That's all I'm asking."

The man uncapped a Chapstick. "They knew, but what can they do?" he asked. "There are only so many carts… so many people driving the carts. The bags will come." He treated his lips and held the Chapstick up to the woman. She shook her head.

"Maybe we should call the kids," she said.

The man put the Chapstick back in his trousers.

"I don't want them to worry," she said louder.

"No news is good news," he said.

The woman inhaled deeply. When she exhaled, her

lips made a little popping sound. She looked down at her feet. "That's how it is with you, isn't it?" She looked up and seemed ready to say something else, but the man was delivering a two-finger salute toward a young lady wearing a gray peacoat. The coat flared at her hips. She was as tall as a model, and while rummaging through her handbag, looked up briefly and smiled at the man. She nearly tripped over a zigzagging toddler and then continued on toward a counter and a bank of phones at the far end of baggage claim.

"Who's that?" the woman asked.

"She was on our plane."

"I don't remember her."

The man didn't speak. He and the woman watched the young lady as she clipped along, her auburn ponytail swinging like a pendulum.

"See, she's going to talk to somebody," the woman said. "Didn't get her bag either, I bet."

"Maybe."

"You two seemed pretty chummy."

"We were in line for the bathroom."

The woman tilted her head up to him — a quizzical look.

"On the plane," he said. You were sleeping."

"Until you lambasted me with your elbow."

"I didn't *lambast* you," he said. "You always use that word."

"Don't use it if you don't like it, but it's my word and

I'm going to grow old with it." She stepped to the edge of the carousel and examined a bag that had circled by several times. She shook her head and flipped the baggage tag as if she were discarding a cigarette butt. She walked back to face the man. "They're lost."

The man was silent. He looked around, then peered at his boots. "If you packed light, we wouldn't always have to check the bags." He grasped an imaginary suitcase by the handle and pantomimed a struggle.

She slapped his hand. "Always the jokester."

"I wasn't joking."

"My suitcase wasn't that heavy."

"I know."

"Then you were joking."

"I was pretending, but I wasn't joking."

"Pretending, joking, whatever. Stop it, please. It's not funny."

"Aye, Captain." He smiled and offered the same two-fingered salute he'd given the young lady.

"*You* checked a bag," she said with a little upturn to one side of her mouth.

"No sense waiting for only one bag."

The woman moved to face the man. The tips of her shoes touched the tips of his boots. She was short and wide; some might say sturdy. She looked up at his eyes. He looked over the top of her head, his line of sight grazing her widow's peak. On each side of his face, a dimple puckered within the gray stubble as he grinned.

She frowned. "I'll tell you what's funny." She licked her fingers and smoothed his wild eyebrows and the silver wings on the sides of his balding head. "You look like a rockhopper penguin. That's what's funny." She examined her handiwork. "You stay here," she said. "I'm going to talk to somebody."

"Wait. There's one," he said. "I think that's yours."

"It's not mine. The pull strap is missing."

The woman started walking through the crowd.

The man called after her. "No, I'm sure that's your old bag. It's a classic."

The woman spun around and returned in sharp, mincing steps. "Do you ever listen to me?" She pointed to the carousel. "I checked it. It's been by five or six times, and every time it comes by, the pull strap is still missing. I wish it was my old bag. If it was, we could finally call Jim and Trish to pick us up, sing carols with the girls back at their house, and forget all about this horrid day."

"Hey, I wasn't the one who set the alarm for *p.m.*" His voice rose. "Remember?"

"And this isn't *my* coffee all over my coat. *Remember?*"

"If you'd put the coat in the overhead bin — "

"I was cold!" The woman pulled at her coat. She looked around and shuffled her feet. "You'd think they could spare a blanket."

A few passengers stared at the man and the woman and then returned to their own conversations, their own shifting stances, as they waited for their bags. The man stared at the carousel for a few seconds and then lifted his chin toward the lonely bag without the strap. "I'm sure that's yours."

The woman groaned, ran after the bag as it curved past, and heaved it off the carousel. When he joined her, she examined the tag.

"Well?" he said.

"Pah! Jennifer Booth." She straightened up. "Am I Jennifer Booth? Do I look like a Jennifer Booth?"

"I'm Jennifer Booth," a younger woman said. Twenty feet away, she waved as if hailing a cab. She wore a navy skirt-suit, and she had round eyes and a sweet smile, which seemed to draw the man's attention.

He adjusted the satchel's strap across his chest, pulled up the suitcase handle, and rolled it to where she stood.

His wife followed.

"Thank you so much," the young woman said, and then leaning around to his wife, "It's dreadfully heavy. I'm surprised you could lift it without help." She clipped a strap to her bag and looked up at a sign: RESTROOMS it said. "Well, Merry Christmas." Her smile beamed in the man's direction, and she tugged the bag away on its chattering wheels.

The man watched her go. "Merry Christmas!"

"No fool like an old fool," his wife said.

"What's your problem?" the man asked. "I smiled at

her. She smiled at me. It was a wonderful experience. It felt festive."

"Well, there she goes," the woman said. She pulled her carry-on from his grip. "Run after her. Run away with her and live in her festive world. She has her bag."

"I would, but I don't have mine. It'll be along though."

"How long are you going to wait?"

"Not much longer, I'm sure."

"You can't just ignore it. Our bags aren't coming."

The man didn't say anything. While rocking back and forth, heel to toe, he watched the carousel. The woman removed her coat and draped it over one arm. She fluffed the back of her hair where it curled at her collar, smoothed her holiday vest, and looked around. Couples pushed strollers, parents dragged crying children, and young teenage girls — bleary-eyed, dressed in sweats — flopped in their fuzzy slippers toward the exits. With each refusal for assistance, skycaps nodded and smiled. Without looking at the man, the woman said, "I know one thing." She raised her chin a tad. "If my pee looked like pink champagne, I'd get it checked out. No ifs, ands, or buts. I wouldn't wait one minute."

"Don't say — " An announcement started. The man winced and spoke louder. "Don't say 'ifs, ands, or buts.' You always say that."

"You should talk to somebody. You never see anybody about anything."

"It's nothing, probably — "

"Or it's something!"

"Probably something I ate."

"It's been a full week."

"And you can stop checking. I'm careful about flushing now."

The woman looked overhead as the stiff male voice finished the announcement. "What did he say?" she asked. "Did he say something about our flight?"

"It's mostly gone anyway."

The red beacon above carousel five twirled and flashed, and a refreshed collection of passengers gathered about the loop. A line of bags careened down the belt. "I'm sure this is ours," the man said. He eyed the bags as they tumbled onto the carousel or coursed around the oval loop. After a few people had retrieved their bags, the man said, "There's the young lady from our flight. I guess she came back."

The young lady shrugged off her peacoat and then turned to search the faces of passengers standing three deep around the conveyor.

"Oh, yes, your bathroom buddy." The woman shifted her heavy coat to the other arm.

"Let me hold that for you," he said.

"I can hold it." She shifted the coat back to the arm away from him.

"I don't know why you brought that thing," he said. He walked around and took her coat.

"It was for Denver in case we missed our connection. You spend a lot of time in bathrooms these days."

"It's the coffee."

"It's your damn prostate."

The man narrowed his eyes, and then pointed to her carry-on. A magazine protruded from an elastic pouch. "Is that what *Vanity Fair* says?"

"No, Barry had the same problem," she said.

The man was silent.

"I talked to Margie." The woman took her coat back from the man and put it on. She wore it like a burden. "Of course, it's been five years since Barry went through all that stuff. He was very lucky. Caught it in time. There are probably even better tests now. Everything's better. Margie says they use lasers or robots or something. Robots? Can you imagine? They're very, very careful about the nerves."

"There's nothing to catch."

"He's taking pills."

"Once you cut the wires, a pill isn't going to help. Not even a horse pill. I know a thing or two about wires." The man gave the woman a long, daring look. She seemed to sag under the heavy coat.

"Layer," he said.

"What?"

He stepped back, holding the open lapels of his jacket like a man in an L. L. Bean catalogue. The woman pulled her coat tight around her. He turned his palm up and began to count fingers. "One — you're more comfortable. Two — you pack lighter. Three — we don't have to check a bag." Then he balled his fingers into a fist and shoved his fist in his pants' pocket.

"You and your layering," she said. "You just go see somebody and I'll ditch the coat."

The man stared across the carousel, the muscles in his jaw pulsing. He gestured ahead and said, "See? She must have had a second bag."

The young lady from their flight was hugging the waist of a young man who wore jeans and a striped rugby shirt. She was pointing at a bag on the carousel. The young man lunged between passengers for a duffel bag, wrestled it off the conveyer with an exaggerated grimace, and smiled.

"There you go," the man said. "I'm sure ours will be right along."

"See how her husband smiled?" the woman said. "You missed your chance."

The man was staring at the young couple.

"Are you even listening to me?" the woman said.

"He's not her husband."

"Her boyfriend, then."

"Her brother."

"It doesn't matter. My point is — "

"She lost her husband."

The woman's mouth went slack. She looked at her

husband. He was still staring at the young man and the young lady.

"Breast cancer," he added.

"She has breast cancer?"

"No, he did. That's what he died of."

"She told you that?"

"Strange, isn't it?"

"When?"

"About a year ago."

"I mean when'd she tell you?"

"I already said. We were in line for the john."

"Waiting for the bathroom and she tells you her husband died of breast cancer?"

"We waited for some time. One thing leads to another. You know how it goes. Just seemed like she wanted to talk."

"What'd you say?"

"What could I say? Nothing. I just listened until it was my turn to use the bathroom. I offered to let her go first."

They both watched the young man hold up the young lady's coat while she slipped her arms through the sleeves. It appeared to be a heavy coat, but not as heavy as the woman's.

"I'd have told her I was sorry," the woman said.

"Sorry for what?"

"Not like an apology 'sorry.' Sorry like I feel bad for her. I can't imagine what she must be going through."

"She seemed okay. It was over a year ago."

"That's the thing. You were a stranger. She might hide some things from a stranger."

The man nodded. "Maybe."

The young lady looked around as if searching for the exit. She noticed the man and waved, and then before turning to leave, she waved again and mouthed "Thank you." The man waved back, as did his wife, and she smiled — not a serene thank-you smile like her husband had offered, but the kind of brave, almost teary, smile you sometimes see exchanged at the airport between parting lovers, not the kind of smile you'd direct at a stranger.

After the young lady left, they stood in silence for many more minutes, the husband and wife, shifting from side to side in the eddy of carousel five as other passengers flowed around them.

"You think they're in Denver?" she asked. "Our bags, I mean." She said this with a fixed gaze as if looking through the baggage carousel to the other side.

"Who knows? They could be anywhere."

The wife didn't look away from the carousel.

"You can get a new bag," he said.

"I don't want a new bag," she said. "All those zippers and pockets."

"Well, then," he said.

With a hitch still in his step, he took her elbow. Next to the men's room, they came to a row of molded orange chairs. He told her to sit. He removed his satchel and handed it to her. She guarded it on her lap. A few men entered the restroom after her husband, and the same men exited. With her thumb she picked at the satchel's tarnished, brass clasp.

When he finally came out, he stood before her. She handed him the satchel. He slung it over his head and leaned in. He paused there, a hand on her shoulder, his mouth near her ear. She stroked his temples, and then he said something only she could hear.

THREE STRIDES TO THIRTY

In March I kept a promise and drove out to the greyhound track in Phoenix. Most of my sadness was sixteen hundred miles behind me in Iowa, evaporating with the rain that had muddied the road to my place. That was my hope at least.

When I pulled into the entrance of the Phoenix Greyhound Park, I gawked like any other rubbernecking tourist. The grandstand looked bigger than I remembered from watching simulcasts at Meskwaki's with Darlene. The whole front was glass, forty feet high if it was ten. Inside, five or six tiers of dining tables with TVs ran the length of it for almost a football field. It was 5:30 on a Friday night, about two hours before the first post. The place was nearly empty except for down front where a small group listened to Sharon, the gal with the big red teardrop earrings who was giving a greyhound adoption tour. That tour was the reason I come early.

It was almost an hour later when a scrawny little security guard stopped me while I was running down the track. He led me into the lady manager's office, the one in charge of the whole place. Nice enough lady. After the commotion I'd caused, I was sucking air pretty good, and she had the guard get me some water. As I was gulping it down, she pointed at my bare feet or maybe the sand I'd tracked onto her carpet and then looked up to say something, but the guard cut her off. "Sorry, Sharon's bringing his shoes," he said.

Her office was on the top level, one up from the grandstand. She told me to take a seat in front of her desk, and then the two of them huddled by the big picture window. I could see the sun setting fast behind 'em.

There wasn't much to the room — an old oak desk with a couple picture frames and a desk lamp, two wooden chairs including the one I was in, and a three-drawer metal file cabinet. It was almost like she'd either just moved in or was getting ready to pack it up. And there were these large photographs on the walls. Other people's memories for sure, framed up real nice: greyhounds in profile wearing racing silks and their owners and trainers standing or kneeling. Usually they held a blue ribbon and smiled into the camera. They had smiles so big you expected they'd stay that way forever.

After those two were done whispering, the guard moved off behind me. Kind of reminded me of Barney Fife on that old Andy Griffith TV show. The manager sat herself down on the front edge of her desk and folded her arms. Said her name was Mrs. Stanton. Then she asked me mine, and I told her.

"Mr. Jensen," she said. "You want to explain why you were out running on the track?"

I guess it didn't sink in at first. I was still thinking about my Darlene and those Arizona magazines of hers and what she had said last fall about not having to own the land.

"Mr. Jensen?" she said again. "What was going on out there?"

Unwinding that one would take a while, so I kept it simple.

"Ma'am, I'll tell ya. It was just something I had to do."

"You took the adoption tour with Sharon, right?"

"Yes ma'am."

"Well, I'm sure she told you to stay off the dog track,"

"Not exactly," I said. "I mean, she didn't say as much, but I kind of figured."

"You thinking of adopting a greyhound, Mr. Jensen?"

"No ma'am."

We sparred back and forth from there, and I could tell she'd been through this routine a time or two. She stood, measuring me up and down with her eyes like a hog buyer at auction, and then walked around to her chair.

"Look," she said. "We get some crackpot running down the straightaway every couple years. I appreciate you at least doing it with your pants on."

I wasn't looking to win the blue ribbon for the craziest old coot she'd ever dealt with, although, if she'd seen me the week before, back in Iowa and running out the front of Don Hendrickson's place, drunk and half asleep in the middle of the night, she might have given me the Tama County prize.

Age-wise Mrs. Stanton was about forty, and she was a big gal. She had on this long black skirt and a vest with a pattern like I'd seen on Indian rugs in Darlene's magazines. Around her neck hung a silver and turquoise necklace that would have tipped my Darlene onto her forehead. She straightened her vest and smoothed the wrinkles in her skirt before sitting down in her high-back chair. She leaned forward to rest her elbows on the desk, and the vinyl squealed.

"Now, at a minimum," she said. "I'm going to boot you out to Washington Street, and I don't want you ever coming back. But I have a problem. Ernie here tells me you had nothing in your pockets. Other than being a little dusty from your run, you were clean."

"That's right, ma'am," I said.

"No keys, no wallet, no coins, no nothing?"

"No, ma'am."

"Well see that's the problem," she said. "If any of that

stuff is down in the sand and one of those greyhounds trips on it, they could break a leg."

"I left all that stuff in my truck," I said. "Except for a little cash I had in my sock."

She slid her thumb back and forth behind her necklace, eyeballing me before she asked, "Mr. Jenson, where are you from?"

"Iowa, ma'am," I said.

"You ever been here before? I mean here in Phoenix."

That kind of made me smile. I wanted to tell her yes, but instead I told her the real truth of it. "No, I've always been in Iowa."

"What do you do back there?"

"Farming," I said. "Corn and soy mostly."

She leaned back into her chair and put her hands behind her head.

"Look," she said. "I'd like to trust you. We've got the first post in about an hour. Delaying things while my lead-outs pick through the sand looking for junk from your pockets is going to piss off the crowd. Why don't you tell me what this is all about? Maybe we can forget the trespassing charge."

Shoot, I didn't want her calling the police, but more than that, I didn't want her banning me from the track. So I figured it was best to tell her most everything. Maybe she'd change her mind.

~

Ma'am, I'll tell you what happened. About five months ago, Darlene, that's my wife, had surgery. Imagine, fifty-eight years old and just gonna have a gallbladder out with one of those new laparoscopy things. Bunch of little holes is all it was supposed to be. From the doctor's face I could see right off that something more was going on. Said it was her pancreas. Hell, I didn't know anything about a pancreas except we all had one. What I know now is when that little sucker gets the cancer, there ain't no hope. At least not for my Darlene. It was everywhere the doctor said. All he could do was sew her up. We spoke to some other doctors about chemo, and in a few days we left the hospital in Iowa City and was back on our farm near Tama.

Been living there ever since we married out of high school. I met her when she moved to town our junior year. She had polio, something you don't see much now. Pitiful, her left leg. Looked like all the air had been let out of it. She wore a brace back then, and between that and her glasses, she was a target. I remember early in that first year, Skeeter Hickman — a real low-life leading a bunch of his low-life friends — comes running up to her locker between classes. He says, "Chester! Marshall Dillon's lookin' for you."

You remember Chester? From *Gunsmoke?* Marshall Dillon's sidekick? The one with the limp? You can see the reruns all night back home. Well, my locker was around the corner. I heard it all. When I stepped out I must have looked like one of those cartoon bulls with steam pouring out its nose. Skeeter didn't say a word. He just took off like the smart-ass mouse he was.

Darlene closes her locker and looks up at me. "Harlan," she says, "thank you, but I know how to handle his type. I don't need a lineman on the football team watching out for me." Shoot, up to that point I didn't think she knew who I was, and it gave me a little boost to ask her out, which I did three weeks later.

I couldn't name you five of the other movies we ever saw, but I remember that first one. It was the only picture showing over at the Strand and hardly a romantic one — *The Great Escape.* Saw it in the afternoon, then took a drive down to Deer Creek. That became a favorite spot of ours over the years. She loved the irises and cattails and the big maples shading the water. Walking along the bank was good exercise for her leg she said. Our first time there, we found a little clearing under a maple where the creek widened into a pond. We stopped and talked and skipped stones until there was just enough light to get back to the truck. I know that sounds corny, but that's the way we were. We sat under that tree like best friends and she opened up about the polio.

She was only six when her mama ran her off to the doctor for a spinal tap. Said it felt like the doctor was driving a wooden stake into her back. Later on, there was months of therapy. Her little muscles stretched until she thought they'd rip apart, and hot wool wraps scalded her leg. And, of course, all the teasing in school. I remember saying, "Darlene, I don't see how you put up with all you been through."

And she says, "I'm like those soldiers trying to escape from that prison camp. I just keep digging."

For a high school girl, she had an older way about her.

After we married, she kept on digging: Ran the house, had a little fruit and flower stand at the market on weekends, and got around with only her cane or nothing at all. Then about twenty years ago, the polio started gnawing at her for more attention. Her left leg began hurting real bad, and her right leg gave out on her. The doctor called it post-polio something or other; told her she'd have to slow down. She pulled the brace and crutches out of the closet. Doctor said the cold weather might make the pain worse. He was right. There was many nights she'd soak in a hot tub. Afterward, I'd soften the calluses of my hands with a little baby oil and try to rub the pain out of her legs while she lay in bed wrapped in that thick pink robe of hers.

For her birthday, her aunt Rita, who lived in Tucson, sent a subscription to *Arizona Highways* magazine. That first issue sprung something inside her. One night while I was trying to fall asleep, I hear her whisper, "Harlan."

"Yeah," I said, trying not to rouse too much.

"Look at this," she says. "Look at the colors in this mountain. We've got to go there someday."

I felt the weight of her leaning into my side of the bed and heard the magazine rustling in my ear.

"Can't this wait till morning?" I said.

"It'll only take a second," she says.

Yeah, she was a hundred and ten pounds of pure determination. I knew where this would end. I reached over, switched on the lamp, and put on my reading glasses. She scooted in real close, then started from the beginning, being careful not to crease the pages except for the little triangle she turned down on the places she wanted to visit. That "second" she'd told me it'd take, turned into a half hour. Getting off to sleep at night always took a little longer whenever a new issue arrived.

I renewed it every year for her birthday, and she folded the corners on all those pictures of red-walled canyons, giant saguaros, and desert sunsets. Boy, those sunsets can call to you when you're staring at another Iowa winter creeping over the horizon. Sure did Darlene.

I promised her we'd get out here someday, but I tell ya, life on a farm don't give you much time away. We were lucky to just get over to Meskwaki. Most every Friday night during winter, if the roads were clear, we picked up the Hendricksons, Don and Evelyn, and headed the ten miles down Highway 30 to the casino, settled in front of one those big screens, and watched the action running right here in Phoenix. They ran simulcasts from Florida and Texas, but like I said, Darlene had a thing for Arizona.

I tell you, she loved those dogs, too, and I don't mean like the gamblers. A young couple brought their greyhound to the casino all the time. She'd catch up with them after they watered him behind the Dairy Queen, stroke his ears back and say how sweet his eyes were. On Saturday afternoons, she'd sometimes take a break from her flower stand and sneak over to our little library on Siegel Street and read about 'em. Then later, about half way through dinner she'd say something like, "Did you know a greyhound can see a moving butterfly at a quarter mile?" She was an expert.

We weren't big bettors, none of us. Maybe two bucks on a quiniela a couple or three times, but it was mostly just a fun night out: pizza, a few beers — Darlene cut hers with Sprite — and we'd tell stories on each other. I gave her plenty of ammo. Seems like most of her stories ended with me covered in mud or manure. We'd all laugh 'till someone peed or farted. Then, we'd laugh even harder. Like a little bird, her laugh.

So one night, about a year ago, we're watching the greyhounds, finishing up our second round of beers, and Don asks, "Darlene, when you going to get Harlan here to take you to Arizona?"

"Once our farming days are over, I suspect," she says.

Don says something wise like, "Prices keep dropping and we may all be headed there soon." Then he says, "So, where's the first place you're gonna go."

She looks up at the TV just as the dogs come busting

out of the gate. Then she points at the screen. "That's my first stop," she says. "Right there along that rail."

I was watching her when she said it, and she had a look like she was there already.

Don says, "Well, looks like you'll have the best seat in the house unless you want to ride one bareback."

She doesn't look at Don. I can see the dogs running in the reflection of her glasses. She says, "No...but I'll tell you what I would like to do."

Then she goes into this story, like we're all kids again sitting around a campfire, believing anything is possible. She talked about wanting to be down on the track. I mean right there where she could get the sand between her toes. Wanted to be there when that fuzzy little bone came whirling by and the gates tripped open. Said those dogs would come charging at her, folding near in half, then stretching out so long like they was leaping across the Grand Canyon. 'Bout this part of her story, she closes her eyes and says, "In three strides they'd hit thirty miles per hour and be by me."

I could imagine that moment with her; kind of feel the wind that swirled off their hard, sleek bodies pass right through her. Except for her leg, she was just like those dogs: taut of muscle and spirit, with such a softness in her eyes. And if you dangled a challenge in front of her snout...Well, she'd be on it. Her mama said she used to run like a jackrabbit. I'm sure she missed running more than she let on.

Come September, before her belly pain started, Darlene got serious about Arizona. This was one of those fall nights that can fool you into thinking the first snow might hold off until you can hang the new calendar on the fridge, and she was out on the porch, bundled up, swaying on our love-seat rocker with an *Arizona Highways* resting on her lap. For the last couple days, she'd been feeling worn out. Thought maybe she'd overdone it.

I'd been cleaning up the kitchen after making Swiss steak. When I come out, she was bathed in yellow porch light. I sat down next to her and she says, "This is what I want to do."

"What?" I said.

"Sell the farm and sit under the stars in Arizona," she says.

"You got stars here," I said.

"These stars are colder. I'm tired...I'm tired of being cold," she says.

"You've never been to Arizona," I said. "How do you know you'll like it?"

"Oh, I've been there," she says. And then she pats the magazine.

Now, we don't have a big farm, but it's been in my family forever, and I promised my parents, rest their souls, that I'd run it after my brother and sister took off for bigger jobs in the city. I don't suppose you've ever lived on a farm, Mrs. Stanton. You've probably not seen dew on a corn crop or pumped the handle of a well or tasted the coolest, most delicious water in the world as it slides down your throat at the end of an August day.

Shoot, I should have known something wasn't right with her. I'm not sure she knew. All I can say now is that Darlene wasn't one to head to the high grass when things got tough. Wish now I would of promised right then, right while we were rocking on the porch, to pack up the truck in a day or two and head down here to take a look.

Instead, I walked over to the porch rail. The corn was in, and the wind was working in my favor that night. All I could smell was dried husks and cool air, the smell of all the autumns I'd ever known.

So I said, "You remember Deer Creek?"

"I remember we've walked those banks more than a few times," she says.

"Anything else?"

"I remember the silver maples and the wild iris....and...I remember a muscular eighteen-year-old farm boy I gave myself to. I'm still seeing him you know."

"That's a lot to give up," I said.

She gathered her crutches and limped over to me. I could tell she didn't want me stopping her. "Harlan," she says, "You don't have to own the land to own the memories."

That one really stuck with me. She was right. Turned it over in my head all the way out here. But we weren't even sixty. I figured there was time. So, I put my arm around her and promised — again — someday soon we'd take a trip to Arizona and see what all the fuss was about. Three weeks later she was getting her gallbladder checked out.

That girl of mine…if she hadn't had bad luck, she'd 'a' had no luck at all. Course she didn't see it that way. "I got you," she said. "That's all the luck I need."

She felt okay until we tried the chemo. She called it the poison. Hell, that was like trying to stop a charging bull with a pellet gun. The cancer kept charging, and the drugs made her puke till I thought she'd puked out every- thing but the cancer. We all knew there was no being a hero on this one. Doctor agreed. Staying at home might be the best thing.

So, I told Darlene that when she recovered from the chemo, I was taking her to Arizona. Not long after we started planning our trip, she entered the hospice. You might say in three strides her cancer hit full speed. But we kept on planning — through the pain that was busting her bones, right up till more morphine than blood was running through her veins. One night she said, "I want you to go. Come back and tell me all about it." I'd have carried what was left of her in my arms right then if I could. I knew she didn't mean while she was alive, but later, when I'd be bawling in front of a marble tile that guarded her bronze urn at the church. She died on a Friday, the first one in January.

A house used to two people don't get half as quiet when there's only one around. There's no sound at all. I had enough loneliness to fill a silo, and it weighed a ton. She was gone, but she was everywhere. The smell of her soap. That little laugh of hers. Her crutches. The baby oil. A closet full of clothes with her pink bathrobe hanging on the hook. And all those magazines lined up on a shelf in the cellar. I couldn't get rid of any of it. I tried to keep busy like our lady pastor said to do. But I'd be out tinkering with one of my tractors, changing filters or some such thing, and feel normal for a few minutes. Then I'd remember and feel worse.

Evelyn and some other folks brought over hot dishes. Don turned up most every day to make sure I was still alive. Sometimes after dinner, if I ate dinner, I'd drive to the church and press my hand to the cold wall with Darlene's name on it. Tell her how much I missed her. Tell her she deserved better after all she went through. Tell her she deserved better than me. Nights, I mostly drank beer and stared at reruns on the TV. I was stuck pretty deep.

Last week, I stumbled over to the Hendricksons for dinner. It would have been Darlene's birthday. The rain had let up that morning and the sky was clear and cold. After downing a couple beers, I left the truck at home and walked the half mile to their house with a six-pack under my arm. I knew what I was doing. Along the way I had two more. When Evelyn answered the door, I stepped in and plopped the remaining four on the dinner table. I popped the top off one and offered it to her. She scorched me a look, so I took a long draw on the beer myself and asked, "Where's Don? I hope not in the bathroom. That's where I'm headed."

I admit, I had a little too much to drink that night. Don tried to slow me down through dinner, but he couldn't deny me my own beer. Evelyn got fed up with my drunken moping some time after coffee and peach pie. She said she was turning in and suggested I do the same. "Harlan," she says, "I know this has been tough on you, especially today. God knows, I miss her, too. But don't you think it's time to put an end to your mourning days? It's been three months."

I said something smart, like: "You're right, Ev. My mourning days are over, but my mourning nights stay open till dawn."

She began to say something but stopped.

Don and I were sitting at the table. I tipped my beer to Ev. She walked over to me, points a finger, and says, "Promise me, you'll at least cut back on the drinking."

"Sure!" I said. "Cross my heart. Just like I promised Darlene we'd go to Arizona."

Evelyn looked at Don like she was asking permission to shoot an old cow, then she marched off to her bedroom. Don slapped a hand on my shoulder and led me to the davenport. He walked off to the kitchen and returned with two more beers. "Might as well finish 'em off," he says. "We're past harm now." He handed one to me and then turned on the television before he sat down in his easy chair.

Sometime after midnight I woke up hearing gunshots. It was Marshall Dillon on TV. He's standing over a body sprawled out in the dirt. Then they showed Chester sitting in a rocking chair outside the jailhouse. He gets out his harmonica and rifles through a few notes. Then he sings:

Run, rabbit, the dog's gonna get you.
Run, rabbit, run. You gotta get away.
Run, rabbit, run. The dog's gonna get you.
Run, rabbit, run. You gotta get away.

Well, I must have been half asleep and the other half drunk, because I just took off. I busted out through Don's front door with him still sleeping in his chair. Must have stumbled a quarter mile down the muddy road to my place, that song in my head, and all these crazy thoughts of greyhounds chasing rabbits and rabbits racing past me, and I don't remember what else except I must have hit a patch of clay, real clay, slick as ice, and I'm flying. Land flat on my back. Lucky I didn't break anything. I'm laying there in that soggy washboard of a road, my clothes soaking up the icy water, and you know what my first thought was? *This'll be a good one for Darlene to tell.* I started sobbing and there was no stopping, until I tried to get up...and farted. Now I was laughing, and crying some

192 | A DRY HEAT

more, and heard my little bird laugh with me. That's
when I noticed the stars — all those cold stars that would
have shined down warm on Darlene in Arizona, at least
for a little while if, well, if I'd been a better husband.

About this time Don pulls up in his truck. He reaches
over and rolls down the window. "Harlan, what in god's
name are you doing? Didn't you hear me calling?" he
says.

All I say is, "I'm going to Arizona."

"Come on," he says. "Just stand up and get in the
truck. I'll drive you home."

He searches the cab front and back and curses 'cause
he's got nothing to cover the seat. As we drive off, I say,
"You remember what Darlene said about wanting to go to
Arizona? Her first stop that Greyhound Park? That's
where I'm going. Arizona. I'm going out there for her."

He didn't try to talk me out of it by running through
all the work I was leaving behind. Truth was, not much
work was getting done anyway. We pulled up to my
house. As I got out, he handed me my coat and said,
"Sleep on it. Come by for breakfast in the morning. If
you're still game, Ev will want to hear about it."

I closed the car door and Don saluted me as he drove
away. I watched him, listening to the gravel pop under his
tires until I realized I was shivering from the breeze
running through my wet shirt. When I turned around,
the porch swing was swaying empty. Well, I tell you,
sleeping on it wasn't going to change my mind.

The next day, I hashed out the details with Don and Evelyn over her special scrambled-egg-and-potato skillet. Ev liked the direction I was heading. I slipped by the church and told Darlene all about it. The lady pastor gave me her blessing. I got some boys from the other farms to keep my place running, and then drove out here in three days with a stack of dog-eared *Arizona Highways* on the seat.

So, that's how I got to Arizona.

Darlene would have loved the greyhound tour. Sharon took about a dozen of us through the paddock. Of course, the dogs were in their crates while those teenage kids sorted the silks for the first race. She talked awhile, and at the end she walked us past the little pool they use to cool the dogs down. The group moved ahead of me. I could see the guy on the tractor creeping along the back-stretch. He looked over his shoulder, checking the surface, I suppose. That's when I wandered toward the starting gates.

No one noticed me at first. Maybe because my trousers looked like the beige ones them kids were wear-ing. With the weight I've lost, they're a little baggy. Anyway, I took my boots and socks off and left them by the gates. Then I walked down the track with my hands in my pockets, thinking about Darlene, thinking about the greyhounds reflected in her glasses. When I reached the spot where I thought the dogs would be after three strides, I stopped and turned around. The sand was cool. I could feel it working between my toes as I shifted my feet. In my mind, those dogs came busting out of the gates, stretching long with each stride. I could see those strides — one, two, three — and I half expected to feel a breeze pass right through me.

That's when someone yelled, "Hey, buddy. You there!"

So I turned, picked up the pace, and before I knew it, I was hauling my ass down the straightaway. Still had my hands in my pockets. I checked back and saw about eight of those kids chasing me. Must have been quite a sight. This big ole boy about as far from the shape of a greyhound as you can imagine being chased by a bunch of young rabbits. I pulled my hands from my pockets and put it into overdrive. If my lungs were screaming, I didn't hear 'em. Then right before turn one, Ernie, your security guard, jumps out of the bushes. Surprised the heck out of me. But it was okay. I stopped and looked back. The guy on the tractor was coming down the straightaway, smoothing my trail. By the next race, he'd have everything all shipshape. Besides, I was done.

That's when everything kind of hit me. I plopped down onto my hands and knees, and between crying and gulping for air, I'm not sure Ernie could understand me. "Do what you gotta do," I told him. "I won't cause you no trouble." He took my arm and walked me off the track. To tell you the truth, I felt so light, he could have carried me up here.

The whole time I'd been going on, the boss lady had been polishing the brass name plate on her desk. When I ran out of things to say, she threw her wadded up Kleenex in the trash. Her eyes were staring in my general direction, but she was focused somewhere else.

"Mrs. Stanton, ma'am, that's about all there is to tell."

Without saying a word, she walked over to the window. She looked down on the track. Then she looked off toward a FedEx jet coming in for a landing. Finally, she took a deep breath. "Mr. Jensen," she said, looking up into the night. "Your wife was quite a woman. There's a lot of truth in what she told you. *You don't have to own the land to own the memories.*" She faced me and leaned back against the windowsill, one arm hugging her waist, her other hand fingering that silver-and-turquoise necklace.

"The memories follow you wherever you go," she said. "Even the hard ones."

She was silent for a moment, and I figured she was waiting for me to say something.

I almost did, but then she cleared her throat. "I hope you found some peace. You can go."

My boots and socks were on a table just outside her office. Ernie waited while I put them on, and then he walked me down to the grandstand. We talked for a minute, and he told me something about Mrs. Stanton. Seems she lost a spouse, too. Damn if a couple years ago in Houston her husband didn't daydream a left turn into a cement mixer.

"That explains a lot," I said.

Ernie shook my hand, told me to take care, and went on back to work.

The grandstand inside had filled up, and there was quite a racket. I found myself a table outside near the rail, close to the starting gates. The waitress twisted up her face when I ordered two beers and a Sprite. I had nothing more to say, so she shrugged and walked off to the bar. The sky was clear, but the lights shining down on the track hid the stars. The night felt cool, mostly because my shirt was still damp from sweat, though not as cool as if I'd been sitting on my porch at home. I pictured Darlene bundled up on our love-seat rocker. It was one of those memories that could go either way. At that moment it weighed on me some. Then the bugle sounded for the first race, and about all of the heaviness lifted.

Mrs. Stanton must have trusted me because the dogs were paraded down the straightaway right on schedule. When the waitress returned, I filled a glass halfway with one of the beers, waited for the head to settle, and then topped it off with the Sprite. After the last dog was led into the gate, the rabbit whirled by, the bell rang, and the gates sprang open.

I raised the glass to Darlene as those greyhounds came charging past. A part of her was down on the track, smoothed into the sand.

It had been easier than I thought: holes in my trousers pockets and a couple of rubber bands to hold her ashes. Like Steve McQueen in *The Great Escape,* I released them as I ran.

If Mrs. Stanton had unraveled what I'd been up to, she hadn't made a fuss. She wouldn't. I think she understood how one day you can be relaxing on a porch making a promise, then in three strides you're flat on your back farting into the cold black night. It's hard to get up.

That was our first stop, Darlene and me. We drove the pages of her *Arizona Highways* for a while, searching out sunsets and warm stars. I had my sad moments. And at times the sadness downshifted into regret, but it had nothing to do with my little sprint down the track. It's just that sometimes there was more riding in my truck than a few magazines and a bronze urn with the rest of Darlene's ashes.

After a couple weeks I called the Hendricksons. Don was out plowing his fields. Ev said it hadn't rained in four days, and the morning frost was letting up. So, we headed home, my little bird and me. It was time to turn the soil and start planting.

RAINBOW TROUT

One fine fall day, a fisherman strolled along the bank of a beautiful river. The day was nearing its end, and he felt content to return to his campsite. The trail through the forest led just past a magnificent pine tree on the edge of the river. Feeling a little tired, he decided to rest for a moment. He removed his cap and fishing vest and carefully placed his fly rod and wading staff against the tree. The soft bed of pine needles offered welcome relief to his aching hip as he sat against the massive trunk and absorbed the magnificent world around him.

The fisherman closed his eyes and smiled at the thought of all the fish he had caught that day, easily his best day ever. He had fished for many years. When he was younger, to catch even one fish in a day was a blessing.

Now he was older, with ten grandchildren, in fact, and could catch a dozen fish or more on an average day.

Years ago, he would keep a fish or two for supper. Now he felt no need, older and wiser perhaps. He enjoyed fly fishing because it was a relaxing contest between the fish and himself. He felt strangely close to them. They were his friends. He took great pride in his ability to skillfully catch and then carefully release each fish back to the river.

This day had been special, even magical. The fishing was effortless, and the rainbow trout more beautiful than he could remember. A river dance of sorts, the trout entertained him by jumping higher and fighting harder than ever before, but once within his reach, they relaxed and welcomed his gentle touch, confident he meant no harm. When he released them, they did not dart away immediately, but rested in the quiet water at his feet until the next performance began.

Rainbow trout, he thought. What a beautiful name for such a beautiful creature. Splashes of yellow, red, and orange graced their sides, the edges blurred, offering no real beginning or end to the colors. Like a rainbow in the sky, they were magnificent to behold, but in a fleeting instant could be gone. A cool breeze brushed his cheek and filled him with a sense of serenity. *Where do they go?* he wondered, as he drifted off to sleep.

When the fisherman awoke, he was surprised at how deeply he had slept. The sun, still low in the sky, assured him that he had only dozed for a few minutes. However, he felt as rested as after ten hours of sleep. He rose to gather his belongings. To the fisherman's amazement, his hip had stopped hurting. He smiled and shrugged, placed his hat on his bald head, and then reached down to gather his gear.

From behind him a voice said, "Excuse me, sir."

Startled, he turned to the river to see a beautiful rainbow trout resting in the calm below. Jokingly, the fisherman asked, "Did you speak to me?"

"Yes," said the rainbow trout.

The fisherman sat down immediately, trying to make sense of the talking fish.

"I know this must be a shock," said the trout, "but I am very happy to finally be able to speak to you."

The fisherman shook his head as if trying to wake up. "Finally able to speak to me! What do you mean? One minute I'm sleeping under a tree and the next? I must be dreaming. I have *never* had a rainbow trout talk to me when I am wide awake."

"We've always been able to talk. Although you could not hear my words as you do now, you were listening. These changes are always so hard to explain."

"What do you mean?" asked the fisherman.

"Yes, you did fall asleep here by the river, but you did not wake up by the same river. You woke up by a river that in many ways looks the same, but in many more ways is better."

"This is all very confusing," said the fisherman. "You make it sound as if I'd died or something."

"Well, that is one of the words used to describe what has happened. It sounds so permanent, though. We rainbow trout do not look at it that way. We prefer the expression 'passed on' because it more closely describes what has happened to you. You have not really stopped living. You have just moved on to the next of what are perhaps many paths in your life."

"I'm still very confused," said the fisherman. "I'm not sure I want to move on if it means leaving my wife, my kids, and my grandchildren. Why now? I'm not very old. There is much I still want to do."

"Easy, easy," the rainbow trout said calmly. "It will all be okay. Let me try to explain. I wish I could answer why you are moving on now, but even rainbow trout do not know that. You have had a wonderful life. You have given more of yourself than many twenty years older than you have given. You have been everything a human is supposed to be — thoughtful, caring, and kind. Through your guidance, you have passed those traits on to your children and grandchildren."

"Yes, but my grandchildren are so young. There is so much I need to teach them."

"Remember," said the trout, "they have your children to help them. You taught your children with skill and patience, and now they will teach their children. Besides, their grandmother has much to offer them as well."

The fisherman was especially saddened by this thought.

"Oh, my poor wife, how will she ever survive?"

"True, this is always difficult, but she has her inner strength and the strength of her family and friends to help her adjust. From what I know of her, she will do well."

The fisherman started to feel a little better. "Then is this heaven?" he asked.

"That depends on you," said the trout. "Is this a place where you could find peace and fulfillment?"

"Well, yes, it is," said the fishermen.

"Then for you this must be heaven," said the rainbow trout. "For others, heaven may be something quite different."

"So, will I be here forever?"

"This is but your next path in life. I'm afraid I do not know any more beyond that."

"All this talk about paths is a little hard to understand," said the fisherman.

"You enjoyed traveling by motor home and went great distances to see the beautiful places my fellow creatures live," said the trout. "You drove on a number of different roads to make your long journey. Your life as a fisherman is like one of those roads. Now, imagine other roads or paths, before and after your Fisherman's Road. Connect them all together, and you have the journey that is you."

The fisherman was standing now, pacing back and

forth, hand on his chin. "Then where did my journey begin and where does it end?"

"Your journey is like a rainbow," said the trout. "It extends beyond where you can see, so I can no better answer your question than to tell you where a rainbow begins or ends."

"How odd. I was dreaming about rainbows as I fell asleep." The fisherman paused for a moment. "So, what happens now?"

"It's all up to you."

That last statement puzzled, then brightened, the face of the fisherman. "You mean I can finally go to Alaska to fish?"

"Anytime, for as long as you want."

"I wish my family could go there with me," the fisherman said, somewhat dejectedly.

"Someday they may," said the trout. "Remember, on any journey your path crosses with others, particularly with the paths of those you love. The paths of your journey and the paths of your family's journey have crossed before, and they will cross again."

"You have been such a comfort to me today. I have not felt such peace since I was a boy when my father would find a way to make all my problems go away. I wish I could console and encourage my family now," said the fisherman.

"Oh, but you can!"

The fisherman removed his hat, rubbed his head, and

sat back down. "Now, I'm really confused. How can I help them? I thought I was out of the picture, and they only had each other."

"Not entirely," said the rainbow trout. "You will be with them always. They may observe a butterfly landing softly on their arm and feel your gentle touch. They may awaken to the mourning doves announcing a summer day and hear your wit and wisdom. They may glimpse a rainbow emerging from the clouds and see your cheerful smile. You left them with wonderful memories, memories that will ease their longing, brighten their days, and inspire them throughout their lives. And at those times, when they feel lost, they may call out to you for advice. Speak to the wind. The wind will carry your message to them. No matter where you are or where they are, you will be close."

The fisherman stared into the water, just the hint of a smile on his face. His father had passed away many years ago. They had often gone fly-fishing together, and he recalled how lonely he'd felt the first time he'd gone fishing alone. His burst of despair had echoed through the forest, then fallen silent; a cool breeze enveloped him in a protective embrace. Every trout that swam past became a reflection of his father. In the trouts' jumps and spins, he witnessed his father's boundless energy. Each time the trusting trout gathered in the shallow pools, he remembered his father's unwavering confidence.

"Yes, I know what you mean," said the fisherman.

"After my father passed away, I always felt close to him while wading these rivers. It was as if your kind could lead me to him."

"I understand," the trout said, "that one of your precious grandchildren gave you the nickname, 'Rainbow Trout.'"

That brought a hearty laugh from the fisherman. He paused and said, "You seem to know so much about me. How can that be?"

He heard a splash and looked up. Circular ripples radiated out from the spot where the trout had been resting. For a few moments, the fisherman gazed at the undulating surface. "Where do they go?" he asked himself and then closed his eyes.

As the fisherman's thoughts flowed with the rippling water, a voice gently interrupted. "Our paths have crossed once more."

Expecting to see the trout, he opened his eyes. His gaze fixed upon a figure that cast a shadow over the river's now-calm surface. The fisherman stood. His face brightened at the sight of an old friend and fellow fisherman, whose soothing words enveloped him in a familiar embrace.

"Welcome home, son," the man said. "It's good to see you again."

BONUS READ

THE FIX-IT MAN
MEMOIR

My father herded my three sleepy-eyed young siblings toward the backseat of our blue Olds '98. I followed him to the car, carrying a cooler with one hand and opening the right rear door with the other.

"Thank you," he said. "You're a gentleman and a scholar and a man of great learning."

We both grinned. He had been feeding me that line since I'd entered high school. It had grown from clever to corny, but we still enjoyed sharing it.

"I'll load the ice chest. Why don't you check with your mom and see if she's ready to go?"

It was August 1970. We were embarking on our annual summer excursion to southern California to escape the Phoenix heat for a week. I was only sixteen but nearly a ten-year veteran of many overland journeys to the Pacific. On those first trips, when my dad's hair was thicker and mine shorter, he would have carried me in my pajamas to the rear bed of a station wagon for our predawn departure. But as we pulled out of the driveway on this morning, I buckled in directly behind him, my wiry frame clothed in cutoffs, a T-shirt, tube socks, and tennis shoes. We traveled north on Interstate 17 for several miles before turning west.

Adjusting the air conditioner vents on the dash, my mother sat up front in the passenger seat. As soon as the sun cleared the horizon, the UV rays pierced the right side of her face, and she opened the vacation with a familiar refrain. "This is the last summer I'm going to spend in this heat." My sister lip-synched the words from the backseat, and then buried her face in a pillow. My two younger brothers, open-mouthed, dozed between us.

I stared out the window and wondered what it would be this trip: alternator belt, vapor lock, air conditioner freezing over. Despite my father's best efforts, mechanical trouble seemed to lie in wait, coiled by the highway, striking without warning, crippling our car in the middle of the desert. Still, I wasn't too worried. The breakdowns all ended the same way: Dad sliding behind the steering wheel and saying, "Looks like I fixed it."

He prided himself on being prepared, a trait he had passed on to me. But I don't think he learned the importance of preparation as an anesthesiologist. I think it was his nature, and it served him well, at home or at work. He had meticulously readied the car for our voyage. Tire pressure, oil level, coolant level, and transmission fluid — they all checked out. Flares, jumper cables, motor oil, antifreeze, extra water, belts, and hoses — just in case. He packed Craftsman tools, an electrician's repair set, and a roll of tape. He seemed to carry two of everything, including a backup to his backup plan.

Our trip officially began on the western edge of town. We raced against the earth's rotation to pass through the Sonoran desert before the sun reached its zenith. From behind my father, I leaned into his reflection and studied his concentration. In a cycle of constant monitoring, his eyes darted behind prescription sunglasses to the instrument panel, the road ahead, and the rear- and side-view mirrors. He drove with both hands on the wheel. I learned later that he employed similar actions every day at work. For ten years he had scanned the ECG, checked the blood pressure, and observed the surgical field. What better cross-training for systematic alertness?

Halfway into our journey we reached a cruising equilibrium. My mom occupied herself with needlepoint. My sister read a book. It had been at least half an hour since either of my brothers had griped, "You're not the boss of me," and they were beginning to doze again.

I stared across the fifty-foot-wide median that divided the highway. Patches of yellow grass and sun-scorched creosote dotted the hard, brown earth. Two crows contested the remnants of a meal. Across the road, saguaros raised their arms to the cloudless blue sky.

Every couple of miles, families in station wagons or sedans, returning to the Valley of the Sun, flew across my field of vision. As we chased our shadow westward, the air conditioner droned.

"What is she...? Oh my God, someone's hurt!" The alarm in my mother's voice tightened my gaze. A young woman wearing a yellow sundress ran back and forth in ten-yard gallops along the median. She was pulling at her black hair; her eyes were wide and her mouth open. We sped past a figure lying still on the ground. "Oh, dear God, Ray! It's a boy! We have to stop!" My dad steered the Olds across the median, turned back east, and parked along the shoulder past a U-Haul truck. A few yards behind us, a Cadillac with a dented hood and grille sat cocked at an angle, partially blocking the inside lane.

"Stay here" was all Dad said. He hurried back across the road to the boy and knelt beside him. My father's hands raced across the motionless figure. He leaned over and pressed his mouth against the boy's mouth. Once, then twice, the child's chest rose. My father straightened and performed stiff-armed compressions against the boy's chest. It was the basic CPR he had shown me when I was in fourth grade. Others were stopping. They rushed from their cars to the boy and back again. I lowered my window. Frenzied pleas penetrated the heat: "Phone... rest stop...ambulance." Another man joined my father. He pushed on the boy's chest while my father resumed the breathing. The boy's mother continued her panicked vigil up and down the barren median, screaming with each exhalation as if she were on fire. My dad and the other man continued, minute after minute. Breathing. Compressing. Breathing. Compressing. I wanted to help, but what could I do?

Suddenly my father stopped, placed his hand along the child's neck, paused, and rose. He walked over to the boy's mother and, with the aid of another man, guided her back to the shade of the U-Haul. He stayed with her for a few minutes, then yielded her care to others.

An elderly man in sunglasses sat erect at the wheel of the Cadillac. His wife sat next to him with her arm across his chest. My father approached the open door, placed a hand on the man's shoulder, and spoke briefly. Through the heat shimmer rising off the highway, Dad trudged back to our car. Dried blood stained his mouth and shirt. He sat down in the driver's seat and stared straight ahead. Gripping the steering wheel, he steadied his hands.

"There was nothing I could do," he began. "I thought I felt a pulse once, but he was like a bag of bones. If he had just looked before he crossed the highway..."

In tight-lipped silence we listened from the backseat as my dad explained, through quivering starts and stops, what he had learned from the mother and the elderly man. The ten-year-old boy had left his wristwatch at the rest stop. His mother made a U-turn across the median and parked her truck along the far side. The boy bounced out of the cab, rounded the front of the truck, and darted across the highway. The Cadillac had hit him at about seventy miles per hour.

At some point we left the scene and pretended to be on vacation. I don't remember where we stayed or what we did, only that the air was thick and salty when we arrived at the motel. My parents shared one room, and we kids split the double beds next door. Sleep didn't come easy for me that night. In the silence and near darkness of the room, I replayed the accident over and over onto the dimpled ceiling. I pictured the boy darting across the highway, one second smiling and confident, then lying twenty yards away, twisted and jelly-limbed the next. I watched my father, my hero, working valiantly to try and save the boy's life. And I saw myself, a mere spectator, confined to the car and my limitations.

Sleep evaded my parents as well. Through the thin wall that separated our rooms and our emotions, I heard my father sobbing. I assumed he was crying because a boy the same age as one of his own had died, because he understood the mother's loss, because the whole thing was preventable. I had never heard him cry before, and it saddened me to know he was hurting, but it also comforted me to know I wasn't alone.

I never asked him about his feelings. At first, I was too

embarrassed, and I didn't want to embarrass him. In a few weeks my young mind moved on to other things. Years later, I followed the genetic pull to medical school and then an anesthesiology residency. During my training and subsequent practice in a community hospital, I confirmed the value of being prepared and having a backup plan. Like most anesthesiologists when faced with a surgical emergency, I adhered to guidelines, initiated algorithms, and borrowed from experience to help steer the patient away from danger.

Yet the art and science of medicine has limits. A few times in the operating room, I peered through the window of those limits at death's inevitability, as powerless to intervene as a sixteen-year-old confined to the backseat of a car in the middle of the desert. But in 1970, my limitations were relative to what I had yet to learn. After my medical training, they were for the most part absolute. The decision trees I adopted branched with life-saving options, including one final, seldom-rehearsed limb available to all physicians: let go, relinquish hope, accept death's tenacious hold.

Coupled to a physician's obligation to provide medical care to the best of his or her ability is the burden to decide when nothing more can be done. I was fortunate. The few times I had to make that decision were within the security of a well-equipped and well-staffed hospital. There I found solace in technology and in the consensus of educated opinion.

Now, I see a more complete picture of my father's grief that August day. When the Cadillac slammed into the boy, it also struck my father. It hurled him beyond his capabilities, far out into death's desert with only his bare hands and a medical degree, where even backup plans are of no use and things can't be fixed. It's a place where gusts of helplessness sting like blowing sand, where the last green vestiges of hope wither under reality's glare, and sense never grows from senselessness.

Editor's note: "The Fix-It Man," originally published in the *Journal of the American Medical Association,* is an autobiographical account of an experience that served as the springboard for the author's novel, *Open Heart.*

ACKNOWLEDGMENTS

Prior to his death in 2020, Gregory D. Williams, M.D. published creative nonfiction and poetry in the *Journal of the American Medical Association*. His fiction appeared in *Blue Mesa Review* and *Elysian Fields Quarterly — The Baseball Review*. His story "What the Doctor Didn't Know" was nominated for the 2010 Pushcart Prize anthology. His story, "Who We Were at Twelve," was awarded the *Arts & Letters* Fiction Prize. The *Bosque Journal* awarded "Comps" its Fiction Prize, and the editor of *American Fiction* chose "Section" for its 2010 edition. The editor gratefully acknowledges the literary magazines that published Dr. Williams' work.

"Comps." *Bosque Journal*. 1st annual issue (October 2011): 39.

"Harvest." *Journal of the American Medical Association*, vol. 292, no. 14, (2004): 1662.

"Rounding the Bases." *Elysian Fields Quarterly: The Baseball Review*, vol. 25, no. 2, (Summer 2008): 62.

"Section." *American Fiction*, New Rivers Press, vol. 11 (2010): 91.

"The Fix-It Man." *Journal of the American Medical Association*, vol. 292, no. 8, (2004): 903-904.

"What the Doctor Didn't Know. *Blue Mesa Review* 21, (Spring 2008): 23.

"Who We Were at Twelve." *Arts & Letters*, vol. 24, (Fall 2010): 9.

ABOUT THE AUTHOR

Gregory D. Williams, M.D. is the winner of Georgia College's 2008 *Arts and Letters* Prize for Fiction. His fiction, essays, and poetry have appeared in *Blue Mesa Review, Elysian Fields, American Fiction, Bosque,* and the *Journal of the American Medical Association.* A graduate of Stanford University and the University of Arizona

Medical School, he grew up in Phoenix, Arizona. Dr. Williams's specialty was anesthesiology, and he was the son of an anesthesiologist. The author passed away in 2020.

ALSO BY GREGORY D. WILLIAMS

Open Heart

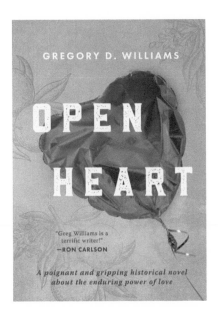

If you enjoyed these stories, read *Open Heart*, a novel about life, death, and growing up.

For other great reads, visit Grand Canyon Press.